VASILISA the BEAUTIFUL
Russian Fairy Tales

Fredonia Books
Amsterdam, The Netherlands

Vasilisa the Beautiful:
Russian Fairy Tales

Edited by
Irina Zheleznova

ISBN: 1-4101-0187-8

Reprinted from the 1966 edition

Fredonia Books
Amsterdam, The Netherlands
http://www.fredoniabooks.com

Contents

Vasilisa the Beautiful

ong, long ago, in a certain tsardom there lived an old man and an old woman and their daughter Vasilisa. They had only a small hut for a home, but their life was a peaceful and happy one.

However, even the brightest of skies may become overcast, and misfortune stepped over their threshold at last. The old woman fell gravely ill and, feeling that her end was near, she called Vasilisa to her bedside, gave her a little doll, and said:

"Do as I tell you, my child. Take good care of this little doll and never show it to anyone. If ever anything bad happens to you, give the doll something to eat and ask its advice. It will help you out in all your troubles."

And, giving Vasilisa a last, parting kiss, the old woman died.

The old man sorrowed and grieved for a time, and then he married again. He had thought to give Vasilisa a second mother, but he gave her a cruel stepmother instead.

The stepmother had two daughters of her own, two of the most spiteful, mean and hard to please young women that ever lived. The stepmother loved them dearly and was always kissing and coddling them, but she nagged at Vasilisa and never let her have a moment's peace. Vasilisa felt very unhappy, for her stepmother and stepsisters

5

kept chiding and scolding her and making her work beyond her strength. They hoped that she would grow thin and haggard with too much work and that her face would turn dark and ugly in the wind and sun. All day long they were at her, one or the other of them, shouting:

"Come, Vasilisa! Where are you, Vasilisa? Fetch the wood, don't be slow! Start a fire, mix the dough! Wash the plates, milk the cow! Scrub the floor, hurry now! Work away and don't take all day!"

Vasilisa did all she was told to do, she waited on everyone and always got her chores done on time. And with every day that passed she grew more and more beautiful. Such was her beauty as could not be pictured and could not be told, but was a true wonder and joy to behold. And it was her little doll that helped Vasilisa in everything.

Early in the morning Vasilisa would milk the cow and then, locking herself in in the pantry, she would give some milk to the doll and say:

"Come, little doll, drink your milk, my dear, and I'll pour out all my troubles in your ear, your ear!"

And the doll would drink the milk and comfort Vasilisa and do all her work for her. Vasilisa would sit in the shade twining flowers into her braid and, before she knew it, the vegetable beds were weeded, the water brought in, the fire lighted and the cabbage watered. The doll showed her a herb to be used against sun-burn, and Vasilisa used it and became more beautiful than ever.

One day, late in the fall, the old man set out from home and was not expected back for some time.

The stepmother and the three sisters were left alone. They sat in the hut and it was dark outside and raining and the wind was howling. The hut stood at the edge of a dense forest and in the forest there lived Baba-Yaga, a cunning witch and sly, who gobbled people up in the wink of an eye.

Now to each of the three sisters the stepmother gave some work to do: the first she set to weaving lace, the second to knitting stockings, and Vasilisa to spinning yarn. Then, putting out all the lights in the house except for a single splinter of birch that burnt in the corner where the three sisters were working, she went to bed.

The splinter crackled and snapped for a time, and then went out.

"What are we to do?" cried the stepmother's two daughters. "It is dark in the hut, and we must work. One of us will have to go to Baba-Yaga's house to ask for a light."

"I'm not going," said the elder of the two. "I am making lace, and my needle is bright enough for *me* to see by."

"I'm not going, either," said the second. "I am knitting stockings, and my two needles are bright enough for *me* to see by."

Then, both of them shouting: "Vasilisa is the one, she must go for the light! Go to Baba-Yaga's house this minute, Vasilisa!" they pushed Vasilisa out of the hut.

The blackness of night was about her, and the dense forest, and the wild wind. Vasilisa was frightened, she burst into tears and she took out her little doll from her pocket.

"O my dear little doll," she said between sobs, "they are sending me to Baba-Yaga's house for a light, and Baba-Yaga gobbles people up, bones and all."

"Never you mind," the doll replied, "you'll be all right. Nothing bad can happen to you while I'm with you."

"Thank you for comforting me, little doll," said Vasilisa, and she set off on her way.

About her the forest rose like a wall and, in the sky above, there was no sign of the bright crescent moon and not a star shone.

Vasilisa walked along trembling and holding the little doll close.

All of a sudden whom should she see but a man on horseback galloping past. He was clad all in white, his horse was white and the horse's harness was of silver and gleamed white in the darkness.

It was dawning now, and Vasilisa trudged on, stumbling and stubbing her toes against tree roots and stumps. Drops of dew glistened on her long plait of hair and her hands were cold and numb.

Suddenly another horseman came galloping by. He was dressed in red, his horse was red and the horse's harness was red too.

The sun rose, it kissed Vasilisa and warmed her and dried the dew on her hair.

Vasilisa never stopped but walked on for a whole day, and it was getting on toward evening when she came out on to a small glade.

She looked, and she saw a hut standing there. The fence round the hut was made of human bones and crowned with human skulls. The gate was no gate but the bones of men's legs, the bolts were no

bolts but the bones of men's arms, and the lock was no lock but a set of sharp teeth.

Vasilisa was horrified and stood stock-still. Suddenly a horseman came riding up. He was dressed in black, his horse was black and the horse's harness was black too. The horseman galloped up to the gate and vanished as if into thin air.

Night descended, and lo! the eyes of the skulls crowning the fence began to glow, and it became as light as if it was day.

Vasilisa shook with fear. She could not move her feet which seemed to have frozen to the spot and refused to carry her away from this terrible place.

All of a sudden, she felt the earth trembling and rocking beneath her, and there was Baba-Yaga flying up in a mortar, swinging her pestle like a whip and sweeping the tracks away with a broom. She flew up to the gate and, sniffing the air, cried:

"I smell Russian flesh! Who is here?"

9

Vasilisa came up to Baba-Yaga, bowed low to her and said very humbly:

"It is I, Vasilisa, Grandma. My stepsisters sent me to you to ask for a light."

"Oh, it's you, is it?" Baba-Yaga replied. "Your stepmother is a kinswoman of mine. Very well, then, stay with me for a while and work, and then we'll see what is to be seen."

And she shouted at the top of her voice:

"Come unlocked, my bolts so strong! Open up, my gate so wide!"

The gate swung open, Baba-Yaga rode in in her mortar and Vasilisa walked in behind her.

Now at the gate there grew a birch-tree and it made as if to lash Vasilisa with its branches.

"Do not touch the maid, birch-tree, it was I who brought her," said Baba-Yaga.

They came to the house, and at the door there lay a dog and it made as if to bite Vasilisa.

"Do not touch the maid, it was I who brought her," said Baba-Yaga.

They came inside and in the passage an old grumbler-rumbler of a cat met them and made as if to scratch Vasilisa.

"Do not touch the maid, you old grumbler-rumbler of a cat, it was I who brought her," said Baba-Yaga.

"You see, Vasilisa," she added, turning to her, "it is not easy to run away from me. My cat will scratch you, my dog will bite you, my birch-tree will lash you, and put out your eyes, and my gate will not open to let you out."

Baba-Yaga came into her room, and she stretched out on a bench.

"Come, black-browed maid, give us something to eat," she cried.

And the black-browed maid ran in and began to feed Baba-Yaga. She brought her a pot of *borshch* and half a cow, ten jugs of milk and a roasted sow, twenty chickens and forty geese, two whole pies and an extra piece, cider and mead and home-brewed ale, beer by the barrel and *kvass* by the pail.

Baba-Yaga ate and drank up everything, but she only gave Vasilisa a chunk of bread.

"And now, Vasilisa," said she, "take this sack of millet and pick it over seed by seed. And mind that you take out all the black bits, for if you don't I shall eat you up."

And Baba-Yaga closed her eyes and began to snore.

Vasilisa took the piece of bread, put it before her little doll and said:

"Come, little doll, eat this bread, my dear, and I'll pour out all my troubles in your ear, your ear! Baba-Yaga has given me a hard task to do, and she threatens to eat me up if I do not do it."

Said the doll in reply:

"Do not grieve and do not weep, but close your eyes and go to sleep. For morning is wiser than evening."

And the moment Vasilisa was asleep, the doll called out in a loud voice:

> "*Tomtits, pigeons, sparrows, hear me,*
> *There is work to do, I fear me.*
> *On your help, my feathered friends,*
> *Vasilisa's life depends.*
> *Come in answer to my call,*
> *You are needed, one and all.*"

And the birds came flying from all sides, flocks and flocks of them, more than eye could see or tongue could tell. They began to chirp and to coo, to set up a great to-do, and to pick over the millet seed by seed very quickly indeed. Into the sack the good seeds went, and the black went into the crop, and before they knew it the night was spent, and the sack was filled to the top.

They had only just finished when the white horseman galloped past the gate on his white horse. Day was dawning.

Baba-Yaga woke up and asked:

"Have you done what I told you to do, Vasilisa?"

"Yes, it's all done, Grandma."

Baba-Yaga was very angry, but there was nothing more to be said.

"Humph," she snorted, "I am off to hunt and you take that sack yonder, it's filled with peas and poppy seeds, pick out the peas from the seeds and put them in two separate heaps. And mind, now, if you do not do it, I shall eat you up."

Baba-Yaga went out into the yard and whistled, and the mortar and pestle swept up to her.

The red horseman galloped past, and the sun rose.

Baba-Yaga got into the mortar and rode out of the yard, swinging her pestle like a whip and whisking the tracks away with a broom.

Vasilisa took a crust of bread, fed her little doll and said:

"Do take pity on me, little doll, my dear, and help me out."

And the doll called out in ringing tones:

"Come to me, o mice of the house, the barn and the field, for there is work to be done!"

And the mice came running, swarms and swarms of them, more than eye could see or tongue could tell, and before the hour was up the work was all done.

It was getting on toward evening, and the black-browed maid set the table and began to wait for Baba-Yaga's return.

The black horseman galloped past the gate, night fell, and the eyes of the skulls crowning the fence began to glow. And now the trees groaned and crackled, the leaves rustled, and Baba-Yaga, the cunning witch and sly, who gobbled people up in the wink of an eye, came riding home.

"Have you done what I told you to do, Vasilisa?" she asked.

"Yes, it's all done, Grandma."

Baba-Yaga was very angry, but what could she say!

"Well, then, go to bed. I am going to turn in myself in a minute."

Vasilisa went behind the stove, and she heard Baba-Yaga say:

"Light the stove, black-browed maid, and make the fire hot. When I wake up, I shall roast Vasilisa."

And Baba-Yaga lay down on a bench, placed her chin on a shelf, covered herself with her foot and began to snore so loudly that the whole forest trembled and shook.

Vasilisa burst into tears and, taking out her doll, put a crust of bread before it.

"Come, little doll, have some bread, my dear, and I'll pour out

13

all my troubles in your ear, your ear. For Baba-Yaga wants to roast me and to eat me up," said she.

And the doll told her what she must do to get out of trouble without more ado.

Vasilisa rushed to the black-browed maid and bowed low to her.

"Please, black-browed maid, help me!" she cried. "When you are lighting the stove, pour water over the wood so it does not burn the way it should. Here is my silken kerchief for you to reward you for your trouble."

Said the black-browed maid in reply:

"Very well, my dear, I shall help you. I shall take a long time heating the stove, and I shall tickle Baba-Yaga's heels and scratch them too so she may sleep very soundly the whole night through. And you run away, Vasilisa!"

"But won't the three horsemen catch me and bring me back?"

"Oh, no," replied the black-browed maid. "The white horseman is the bright day, the red horseman is the golden sun, and the black horseman is the black night, and they will not touch you."

Vasilisa ran out into the passage, and Grumbler-Rumbler the Cat rushed at her and was about to scratch her. But she threw him a pie, and he did not touch her.

Vasilisa ran down from the porch, and the dog darted out and was about to bite her. But she threw him a piece of bread, and the dog let her go.

Vasilisa started running out of the yard, and the birch-tree tried to lash her and to put out her eyes. But she tied it with a ribbon, and the birch-tree let her pass.

The gate was about to shut before her, but Vasilisa greased its hinges, and it swung open.

Vasilisa ran into the dark forest, and just then the black horseman galloped by and it became pitch black all around. How was she to go back home without a light? What would she say? Why, her stepmother would do her to death.

So she asked her little doll to help her and did what the doll told her to do.

14

She took one of the skulls from the fence and, mounting it on a stick, set off across the forest. Its eyes glowed, and by their light the dark night was as bright as day.

As for Baba-Yaga, she woke up and stretched and, seeing that Vasilisa was gone, rushed out into the passage.

"Did you scratch Vasilisa as she ran past, Grumbler-Rumbler?" she demanded.

And the cat replied:

"No, I let her pass, for she gave me a pie. I served you for ten years, Baba-Yaga, but you never gave me so much as a crust of bread."

Baba-Yaga rushed out into the yard.

"Did you bite Vasilisa, my faithful dog?" she demanded.

Said the dog in reply:

"No, I let her pass, for she gave me some bread. I served you for ever so many years, but you never gave me so much as a bone."

"Birch-tree, birch-tree!" Baba-Yaga roared. "Did you put out Vasilisa's eyes for her?"

Said the birch-tree in reply:

"No, I let her pass, for she bound my branches with a ribbon. I have been growing here for ten years, and you never even tied them with a string."

Baba-Yaga ran to the gate.

"Gate, gate!" she cried. "Did you shut before her that Vasilisa might not pass?"

Said the gate in reply:

"No, I let her pass, for she greased my hinges. I served you for ever so long, but you never even put water on them."

Baba-Yaga flew into a temper. She began to beat the dog and thrash the cat, to break down the gate and to chop down the birch-tree, and she was so tired by then that she forgot all about Vasilisa.

Vasilisa ran home, and she saw that there was no light on in the house. Her stepsisters rushed out and began to chide and scold her.

"What took you so long fetching the light?" they demanded. "We cannot seem to keep one on in the house at all. We have tried to strike a light again and again but to no avail, and the one we got from the neighbours went out the moment it was brought in. Perhaps yours will keep burning."

They brought the skull into the hut, and its eyes fixed themselves on the stepmother and her two daughters and burnt them like fire. The stepmother and her daughters tried to hide but, run where they would, the eyes followed them and never let them out of their sight.

By morning they were burnt to a cinder, all three, and only Vasilisa remained unharmed.

She buried the skull outside the hut, and a bush of red roses grew up on the spot.

16

After that, not liking to stay in the hut any longer, Vasilisa went into the town and made her home in the house of an old woman.

One day she said to the old woman:

"I am bored sitting around doing nothing, Grandma. Buy me some flax, the best you can find."

The old woman bought her some flax, and Vasilisa set to spinning yarn. She worked quickly and well, the spinning-wheel humming and the golden thread coming out as even and thin as a hair. She began to weave cloth, and it turned out so fine that it could be passed through the eye of a needle, like a thread. She bleached the cloth, and it came out whiter than snow.

"Here, Grandma," said she, "go and sell the cloth and take the money for yourself."

The old woman looked at the cloth and gasped.

"No, my child, such cloth is only fit for a Tsarevich to wear. I had better take it to the palace."

She took the cloth to the palace, and when the Tsarevich saw it, he was filled with wonder.

"How much do you want for it?" he asked.

"This cloth is too fine to be sold, I have brought it to you for a present."

The Tsarevich thanked the old woman, showered her with gifts and sent her home.

But he could not find anyone to make him a shirt out of the cloth, for the workmanship had to be as fine as the fabric. So he sent for the old woman again and said:

"You wove this fine cloth, so you must know how to make a shirt out of it."

"It was not I that spun the yarn or wove the cloth, Tsarevich, but a maid named Vasilisa."

"Well, then, let her make me a shirt."

The old woman went home, and she told Vasilisa all about it.

Vasilisa made two shirts, embroidered them with silken threads, studded them with large, round pearls and, giving them to the old woman to take to the palace, sat down at the window with a piece of embroidery.

By and by whom should she see but one of the Tsar's servants come running toward her.

"The Tsarevich bids you come to the palace," said the servant.

Vasilisa went to the palace and, seeing her, the Tsarevich was smitten with her beauty.

"I cannot bear to let you go away again, you shall be my wife," said he.

He took both her milk-white hands in his and he placed her in the seat beside his own.

And so Vasilisa and the Tsarevich were married, and, when Vasilisa's father returned soon afterwards, he made his home in the palace with them.

Vasilisa took the old woman to live with her too, and, as for her little doll, she always carried it about with her in her pocket.

And thus are they living to this very day, waiting for us to come for a stay.

Tsarevich Ivan and Grey Wolf

nce upon a time there was a Tsar named Berendei, and he had three sons, the youngest of whom was called Ivan.

Now the Tsar had a beautiful garden with an apple-tree in it that bore golden apples.

One day the Tsar found that somebody was visiting his garden and stealing his golden apples. The Tsar was very unhappy about this. He sent watchmen into the garden, but they were unable to catch the thief.

The Tsar was so grieved that he would not touch food or drink. His sons tried to cheer him.

"Do not grieve, Father dear," they said, "we shall keep watch over the garden ourselves."

Said the eldest son: "Today it is my turn to keep watch."

And he went into the garden. He walked about for a long time but saw no one, so he flung himself down on the soft grass and went to sleep.

In the morning the Tsar said to him:

"Come, now, have you brought me good news? Have you discovered who the thief is?"

"No, Father dear. That the thief was not there I am ready to swear. I did not close my eyes all night, but I saw no one."

On the following night the middle son went out to keep watch, and he, too, went to sleep and in the morning said he had seen no one.

It was now the youngest son's turn to go and keep watch. Tsarevich Ivan went to watch his father's garden and he did not dare so much as to sit down, let alone lie down. If he felt that he was getting sleepy, he would wash his face in dew and become wide awake again.

Half the night passed by, and all of a sudden what should he see but a light shining in the garden. Brighter and brighter it grew, and it lit up everything around.

Tsarevich Ivan looked, and there in the apple-tree he saw the Fire-Bird pecking at the golden apples.

Tsarevich Ivan crept up to the tree and caught the bird by the tail. But the Fire-Bird broke free of his grasp and flew away, leaving a feather from its tail in his hand.

In the morning Tsarevich Ivan went to his father.

"Well, my son, have you caught the thief?" asked the Tsar.

"No, Father," said Tsarevich Ivan, "I have not caught him, but I have discovered who he is. See, he sends you this feather as a keepsake. The Fire-Bird is the thief, Father."

The Tsar took the feather, and from that time he became cheerful again and began to eat and drink. But one fine day he fell to thinking about the Fire-Bird and, calling his sons to his side, said:

"My dear sons, I would have you saddle your trusty steeds and set out to see the wide world. If you search in all its far corners, perhaps you will come upon the Fire-Bird."

The sons bowed to their father, saddled their trusty steeds and set out. The eldest son took one road, the middle son another, and Tsarevich Ivan a third.

Whether Tsarevich Ivan was long on the way or not, no one can say, but one day, it being summer and very warm, he felt so tired that he got off his horse and, binding its feet so that it could not go very far, lay down to rest.

Whether he slept for a long time or a little time nobody knows, but when he woke up he found that his horse was gone. He went to look for it, he walked and he walked, and at last he found its remains: nothing but bones, picked clean. Tsarevich Ivan was greatly grieved. How could he continue on his journey without a horse?

"Ah, well," he thought, "it cannot be helped, and I must make the best of it."

And he went on on foot. He walked and walked till he was so tired that he was ready to drop. He sat down on the soft grass, and he was very sad and woebegone. Suddenly, lo and behold! who should come running up to him but Grey Wolf.

"Why are you sitting here so sad and sorrowful, Tsarevich Ivan?" asked Grey Wolf.

"How can I help being sad, Grey Wolf! I have lost my trusty steed."

"It was I who ate up your horse, Tsarevich Ivan. But I am sorry for you. Come, tell me, what are you doing so far from home and where are you going?"

"My father has sent me out into the wide world to seek the Fire-Bird."

"Has he now? Well, you could not have reached the Fire-Bird on that horse in three years. I alone know where it lives. So be it—since I have eaten up your horse, I shall be your true and faithful servant. Get on my back and hold fast."

Tsarevich Ivan got on his back and Grey Wolf was off in a flash. Blue lakes skimmed past ever so fast, green forests swept by in the wink of an eye, and at last they came to a castle with a high wall round it.

"Listen carefully, Tsarevich Ivan," said Grey Wolf, "and remember what I say. Climb over that wall. You have nothing to fear—we have come at a lucky hour, all the guards are sleeping. In a chamber within the tower you will see a window, in that window hangs a golden cage, and in that cage is the Fire-Bird. Take the bird and hide it in your bosom, but mind you do not touch the cage!"

Tsarevich Ivan climbed over the wall and saw the tower with the golden cage in the window and the Fire-Bird in the cage. He took the bird out and hid it in his bosom, but he could not tear his eyes away from the cage.

"Ah, what a handsome golden cage it is!" he thought longingly. "How can I leave it here!"

And he forgot all about the Wolf's warning. But the moment he

touched the cage, a hue and cry arose within the castle—trumpets began to blow, drums began to beat, and the guards woke up, seized Tsarevich Ivan and marched him off to Tsar Afron.

"Who are you and whence do you hail?" Tsar Afron demanded angrily.

"I am Tsarevich Ivan, son of Tsar Berendei."

"Fie, shame on you! To think of the son of a tsar being a thief!"

"Well, you should not have let your bird steal apples from our garden."

"If you had come and told me about it in an honest way, I would have made you a present of the Bird out of respect for your father,

Tsar Berendei. But now I shall spread the ill fame of your family far and wide. Or no—perhaps I will not, after all. If you do what I tell you, I shall forgive you. In a certain tsardom there is a Tsar named Kusman and he has a Horse with a Golden Mane. Bring me that Horse and I will make you a gift of the Fire-Bird and the cage besides."

Tsarevich Ivan felt very sad and crestfallen, and he went back to Grey Wolf.

"I told you not to touch the cage," said the Wolf. "Why did you not heed my warning?"

"I am sorry, Grey Wolf, please forgive me."

25

"You are sorry, are you? Oh, well, get on my back again. I gave my word, and I must not go back on it. A truth that all good folk accept is that a promise must be kept."

And off went Grey Wolf with Tsarevich Ivan on his back. Whether they travelled for a long or a little time nobody knows, but at last they came to the castle where the Horse with the Golden Mane was kept.

"Climb over the wall, Tsarevich Ivan, the guards are asleep," said Grey Wolf. "Go to the stable and take the Horse, but mind you do not touch the bridle."

Tsarevich Ivan climbed over the castle wall and, all the guards being asleep, he went to the stable and caught Golden Mane. But he could not help picking up the bridle—it was made of gold and set with precious stones—a fitting bridle for such a horse.

No sooner had Tsarevich Ivan touched the bridle than a hue and cry was raised within the castle. Trumpets began to blow, drums began to beat, and the guards woke up, seized Tsarevich Ivan and marched him off to Tsar Kusman.

"Who are you and whence do you hail?" the Tsar demanded.

"I am Tsarevich Ivan."

"A tsar's son stealing horses! What a foolish thing to do! A common peasant would not stoop to it. But I shall forgive you, Tsarevich Ivan, if you do what I tell you. Tsar Dalmat has a daughter named Yelena the Fair. Steal her and bring her to me, and I shall make you a present of my Horse with the Golden Mane and of the bridle besides."

Tsarevich Ivan felt more sad and crestfallen than ever, and he went back to Grey Wolf.

"I told you not to touch the bridle, Tsarevich Ivan!" said the Wolf. "Why did you not heed my warning?"

"I am sorry, Grey Wolf, please forgive me."

"Being sorry won't do much good. Oh, well, get on my back again."

And off went Grey Wolf with Tsarevich Ivan. By and by they came to the tsardom of Tsar Dalmat, and in the garden of his castle Yelena the Fair was strolling with her women and maids.

26

"This time I shall do everything myself," said Grey Wolf. "You go back the way we came and I will soon catch up with you."

So Tsarevich Ivan went back the way he had come, and Grey Wolf jumped over the wall into the garden. He crouched behind a bush and peeped out, and there was Yelena the Fair strolling about with all her women and maids. After a time she fell behind them, and Grey Wolf at once seized her, tossed her across his back, jumped over the wall and took to his heels.

Tsarevich Ivan was walking back the way he had come, when all of a sudden his heart leapt with joy, for there was Grey Wolf with Yelena the Fair on his back! "You get on my back too, and be quick about it, or they may catch us," said Grey Wolf.

Grey Wolf sped down the path with Tsarevich Ivan and Yelena the Fair on his back. Blue lakes skimmed past ever so fast, green forests swept by in the wink of an eye. Whether they were long on the way or not nobody knows, but by and by they came to Tsar Kusman's tsardom.

"Why are you so silent and sad, Tsarevich Ivan?" asked Grey Wolf.

"How can I help being sad, Grey Wolf! It breaks my heart to part with such loveliness. To think that I must exchange Yelena the Fair for a horse!"

"You need not part with such loveliness, we shall hide her somewhere. I will turn myself into Yelena the Fair and you shall take me to the Tsar instead."

So they hid Yelena the Fair in a hut in the forest, and Grey Wolf turned a somersault, and was at once changed into Yelena the Fair. Tsarevich Ivan took him to Tsar Kusman, and the Tsar was delighted and thanked him over and over again.

"Thank you for bringing me a bride, Tsarevich Ivan," said he. "Now the Horse with the Golden Mane is yours, and the bridle too."

Tsarevich Ivan mounted the horse and went back for Yelena the Fair. He put her on the horse's back and away they rode!

Tsar Kusman held a wedding and feast to celebrate it and he

27

feasted the whole day long, and when bedtime came he led his bride into the bedroom. But when he got into bed with her what should he see but the muzzle of a wolf instead of the face of his young wife! So frightened was the Tsar that he tumbled out of bed, and Grey Wolf sprang up and ran away.

He caught up with Tsarevich Ivan and said:

"Why are you sad, Tsarevich Ivan?"

"How can I help being sad! I cannot bear to think of exchanging the Horse with the Golden Mane for the Fire-Bird."

"Cheer up, I will help you," said the Wolf.

Soon they came to the tsardom of Tsar Afron.

"Hide the horse and Yelena the Fair," said the Wolf. "I will turn myself into Golden Mane and you shall take me to Tsar Afron."

So they hid Yelena the Fair and Golden Mane in the woods, and Grey Wolf turned a somersault and was changed into Golden Mane. Tsarevich Ivan led him off to Tsar Afron, and the Tsar was delighted and gave him the Fire-Bird and the golden cage too.

Tsarevich Ivan went back to the woods, put Yelena the Fair on Golden Mane's back and, taking the golden cage with the Fire-Bird in it, set off homewards.

Meanwhile Tsar Afron had the gift horse brought to him, and he was just about to get on its back when it turned into a grey wolf. So frightened was the Tsar that he fell down where he stood, and Grey Wolf ran away and soon caught up with Tsarevich Ivan.

"And now I must say good-bye," said he, "for I can go no farther."

Tsarevich Ivan got off the horse, bowed low three times, and thanked Grey Wolf humbly.

"Do not say good-bye for good, for you may still have need of me," said Grey Wolf.

"Why should I need him again?" thought Tsarevich Ivan. "All my wishes have been fulfilled."

He got on Golden Mane's back and rode on with Yelena the Fair and the Fire-Bird. By and by they reached his own native land, and

Tsarevich Ivan decided to stop for a bite to eat. He had a little bread with him, so they ate the bread and drank fresh water from the spring, and then lay down to rest.

No sooner had Tsarevich Ivan fallen asleep than his brothers came riding up. They had been to other lands in search of the Fire-Bird, and were now coming home empty-handed.

When they saw that Tsarevich Ivan had got everything, they said:

"Let us kill our brother Ivan, for then all his spoils will be ours."

And with that they killed Tsarevich Ivan. Then they got on Golden Mane's back, took the Fire-Bird, seated Yelena the Fair on a horse and said:

"See that you say not a word about this at home!"

So there lay Tsarevich Ivan on the ground, with the ravens circling over his head. All of a sudden who should come running but Grey Wolf. He ran up and he seized a raven and her fledgling.

"Fly and fetch me dead and living water, Raven," said the Wolf. "If you do, I shall let your nestling go."

The Raven flew off—what else could she do?—while the Wolf held her fledgling. Whether a long time passed by or a little time nobody knows, but at last she came back with the dead and living water. Grey Wolf sprinkled the dead water on Tsarevich Ivan's

wounds, and the wounds healed. Then he sprinkled him with the living water, and Tsarevich Ivan came back to life.

"Oh, how soundly I slept!" said he.

"Aye," said Grey Wolf, "and but for me you would never have wakened. Your own brothers killed you and took away all your treasures. Get on my back, quick."

They went off in hot pursuit, and they soon caught up the two brothers, and Grey Wolf tore them to bits and scattered the bits over the field

Tsarevich Ivan bowed to Grey Wolf and took leave of him for good.

He rode home on the Horse with the Golden Mane, and he brought his father the Fire-Bird and himself a bride—Yelena the Fair.

Tsar Berendei was overjoyed and asked his son all about everything. Tsarevich Ivan told him how Grey Wolf had helped him, and how his brothers had killed him while he slept and Grey Wolf had torn them to bits.

At first Tsar Berendei was sorely grieved, but he soon got over it. And Tsarevich Ivan married Yelena the Fair and they lived together in health and cheer for many a long and prosperous year.

The Two Ivans

Once upon a time there lived two brothers, and they were both called Ivan: Ivan the Rich and Ivan the Poor.

Ivan the Rich had bread in the oven and meat on the table, a well-furnished house and a well-stocked stable, bins full of flour and stores full of wheat, and good things to wear as well as to eat. His sheep they were fat, and his cows they were sleek, and they walked in the meadows by a winding creek. In short, he had everything, and no one to care for but himself and his wife. For Ivan the Rich had no children, big or small.

As for Ivan the Poor, he had seven children and nothing to his name save a cat by the fire and a frog in the mire. And all his seven children they sat in a group, and they begged for buckwheat porridge and for cabbage soup. But, alas, there was nothing to give them to eat, not a crust of bread, nor a scrap of meat.

There was no help for it, and so Ivan the Poor went to his rich brother to ask for some food.

"Good morrow, brother!" said he.

"Good morrow, Ivan the Poor! And what brings you here?"

33

"Lend me a bit of flour, brother. You shall have it back, I promise you."

"Very well," said Ivan the Rich. "Here is a bowl of flour for you, and you'll give me back a sackful."

"A whole sack in return for a bowl! What are you saying, brother! Don't you think it's too much?"

"Well, if it is, then don't bother me, but go and beg at someone else's doorstep!"

There was nothing to be done and, with tears rolling down his cheeks, Ivan the Poor took the bowl of flour and went home. But he had only just reached the gate of his house when a gusty Wind began to blow. Shrieking and whistling, he came spinning like a top at Ivan the Poor, blew all the flour out of the bowl and, leaving only a bit on the bottom, flew off again.

Now this made Ivan the Poor very angry indeed.

"Ah, you bad North Wind!" cried he. "You have done my poor children an ill turn, you have left them hungry. But wait and see, I shall find you and make you pay for your mischief!"

And Ivan the Poor set off to catch the Wind. The Wind swept along the road, and Ivan the Poor ran in his wake. The Wind rushed into the forest, and Ivan the Poor hurried after him. They came upon a huge oak-tree, but no sooner had the Wind stolen into a hollow in its side than there was Ivan creeping in with him.

Said the Wind when he saw Ivan the Poor there beside him:

"Come, tell me, my good man, why do you follow me about?"

"I will tell you if you wish to know," said Ivan the Poor in reply. "I was bringing my hungry children a bit of flour, and you, mischief-maker that you are, flew at me and whistled and scattered all the flour. And how can I go back home empty-handed!"

"Oh, is that all!" said the Wind. "Well, there's no need to be so upset. Here is a magic table-cloth for you: it will give you whatever you ask for."

Ivan the Poor was overjoyed. He bowed to the Wind and ran home.

As soon as he reached his house he spread the table-cloth on the table and said:

"Cloth, cloth, magic cloth, let us have something to eat and to drink!"

And no sooner were the words out of his mouth than there appeared on the table-cloth cabbage soup and mushroom pie and a great big ham to cheer the eye.

Ivan the Poor and his children ate till they could eat no more and then they went to bed. And in the morning, just as they had sat down to breakfast, who should come into the hut but Ivan the Rich.

Seeing the table groaning under the weight of the food, Ivan the Rich turned red with anger.

"What is this I see, brother!" he cried. "Have you become rich all of a sudden?"

"Not rich, really. But at least I shall never want for food any more and will always have enough left over to give you a meal too. Oh, and that reminds me. I owe you a sack of flour, don't I? Well, you shall have it back right now. Cloth, cloth, magic cloth, let me have a sack of flour!"

And lo! no sooner were the words out of his mouth than there was the sack of flour on the table.

Ivan the Rich took the flour without a word and left the hut.

But, when evening came, there he was back again to see his brother.

"Do be kind and help me out, brother," said he. "Do not leave me in a fix. I've a full house of people from a rich village come for a visit. and as the stove has not been heated or the bread baked, I have

nothing to feast them with. So, please, lend me your magic table-cloth for an hour or two."

And what did Ivan the Poor do but give him the magic cloth.

Ivan the Rich fed his guests and saw them off and, hiding the magic table-cloth in his chest, he got out another just like it except that it was an ordinary and not a magic cloth, and took it to Ivan the Poor.

"Thank you, brother," said he. "We have dined as well as anyone could wish for."

After a time Ivan the Poor and his children sat down to eat, and they spread the table-cloth on the table.

"Cloth, cloth, magic cloth, let us have some supper!" said Ivan the Poor.

And the table-cloth lay there white and clean and shining but, though they waited patiently, no food appeared on it.

Ivan the Poor ran to his rich brother's house.

"What have you done with my magic table-cloth, brother?" he asked him.

"Whatever are you talking about? Why, I gave it back to you."

Ivan the Poor burst into tears and went home.

A day passed, and another flew by, and his children began to cry and ask for food. And there was nothing at all to give them to eat, not a crust of bread, nor a scrap of meat. It could not be helped, and Ivan the Poor went to see his rich brother again.

"Good morrow, brother!" said he.

"Good morrow to you, Ivan the Poor! What brings you here?"

"My children are crying, they are so hungry. Let me have a bit of flour, brother, or a piece of bread."

"I haven't any flour to give you, or any bread, either. But there's a plate of oat jelly in the pantry. You can have that if you like. It's on the barrel by the door, and don't come back to ask for more."

Ivan the Poor took the plate of jelly and went home. The day was warm, the Sun shone brightly, and his rays fell straight on to the jelly in the plate. The jelly melted, and it all dribbled away. Nothing was left of it but a little puddle in the road.

Ivan the Poor was very angry.

"Ah, you foolish, foolish Sun!" he cried. "It's only a game for you, but it's ill luck indeed for my poor children. I'll find you, and I'll make you pay for your mischief."

And Ivan the Poor set out to catch the Sun. He walked and he walked, but the Sun was always ahead of him, and it was only towards evening that he sank down beyond the mountain. It was there that Ivan the Poor found him.

Said the Sun when he saw Ivan the Poor there beside him:

"Come, Ivan, tell me, why do you follow me about?"

"I will tell you if you wish to know," Ivan the Poor replied. "I was taking some oat jelly home to my hungry children when you, foolish Sun that you are, began to shine brighter and brighter and to play with the jelly. The jelly melted and it trickled all out on to the road. And how can I go back home to my children empty-handed!"

"Oh, is that all!" said the Sun. "I was the one to make you suffer, and I shall be the one to help you. Here is a goat for you from my own flock. Feed it with acorns, and it will give gold instead of milk."

Ivan the Poor bowed to the Sun and drove the goat home. He fed it with acorns and then began to milk it. And instead of milk the goat gave liquid gold.

From that day on Ivan the Poor's life changed for the better and his children always had enough to eat.

When he heard about the goat, Ivan the Rich came running to see his brother.

"Good morrow, brother!" cried he.

"Good morrow to you, Ivan the Rich."

"Do be kind and help me out, brother. Lend me your goat for an hour. I must return some money I owe, and I haven't a kopek."

"Very well, you may take it, but do not try to cheat me again."

Ivan the Rich took away the goat and milked it, and when he had got enough gold and to spare, he hid the goat in a shed and drove an ordinary goat back to Ivan the Poor's house.

"Thank you for helping me out, brother," said he.

Ivan the Poor fed the goat with acorns and then began to milk it, and the milk ran from its udders and down to its hoofs, but not a speck of gold was there anywhere to be seen.

Ivan the Poor ran to his rich brother, but the other would not so much as listen to him.

"I know nothing about it," said he. "I gave you back the very same goat I got from you."

Ivan the Poor burst into tears and went home. The days passed, and the weeks flew by, and his children began to cry with hunger again. Winter had set in, it was very cold, and there was nothing in the house to give them to eat, not a crust of bread, nor a scrap of meat. There was no help for it, and Ivan the Poor went to his rich brother to ask for food.

"My children are crying, they are so hungry, brother," said he. "Do lend me a bit of flour!"

"I haven't any flour or bread to give you, but you can have some of yesterday's cabbage soup. It's in the pantry in a pot, and is a treat when eaten hot."

Ivan the Poor took the pot of soup and went home. He walked along, and there was a crackling Frost out. The wind howled and droned, and it grew colder by the minute. And now the Frost began to play with the cabbage soup. He would spread a film of ice over it first, and then sweep some fine, dry snow over the ice. He played and he played, and he froze the cabbage soup all up. There was nothing left in the pot save a small piece of dark ice on the bottom.

Ivan the Poor was very angry.

"Ah, you bad old Frost, you old Red Nose, my cheeks you nipped and my feet you froze. It's only a game for you, but it's ill luck indeed for my children. Wait and see, I will catch you and make you answer for your mischief!"

And Ivan the Poor set out to catch the Frost. The Frost tore over the fields, and Ivan the Poor trudged after him. The Frost swept into the forest, and Ivan the Poor followed close behind. The Frost lay down under a large snowdrift, and there was Ivan the Poor at his side. Said the Frost in wonder:

"Why do you dog my steps, Ivan? What is it you want of me?"

"Well, if you really wish to know, I will tell you," Ivan replied. "I was taking a pot of yesterday's cabbage soup home to my children, and you started playing your pranks and froze it all up. And how can I go back home empty-handed! My brother took away my magic table-cloth and the goat that gave gold instead of milk, and now you have gone and spoiled the cabbage soup!"

"Oh, is that all!" said the Frost. "Well, to make it up to you, I shall give you a sack-help-me-out-with-a-whack. Say 'Two out of the sack!'—and the two will jump out. Say 'Two into the sack!'—and the two will creep back into the sack again."

Ivan the Poor bowed and went home. He came into the house, took out the sack and said:

"Two out of the sack!"

And lo and behold! two thick cudgels of pine sprang out of the sack and they fell on Ivan the Poor and began to thrash him, saying:

"Ivan the Rich thinks of nothing but gain, learn to be wise or he'll trick you again!"

So hard did they thrash him that it was all Ivan the Poor could do to get his breath back and to cry "Two into the sack!" And at once the two cudgels crept into the sack and lay there very quietly.

Evening had scarcely arrived when Ivan the Rich came running to his brother's house.

"Where have you been, Ivan the Poor?" he asked. "And what have you brought back with you?"

"I paid the Frost a visit, brother, and he gave me a magic sack for a gift. You have only to say 'Two out of the sack!' and the two will jump out and do all that needs to be done."

"Do be kind, Ivan the Poor, and lend me your sack for a day. My roof is all broken, and there is no one to repair it."

"Very well, Ivan the Rich, you may have my sack."

Ivan the Rich took the sack home with him and locked the door.

"Two out of the sack!" he cried.

And lo and behold! two thick cudgels of pine sprang out of the sack. They fell on Ivan the Rich and began to thrash him, saying:

"What belongs to your brother is not for you, give him back his goat and his table-cloth too!"

Ivan the Rich ran to his brother's house, and the two cudgels flew after him, beating and thrashing him soundly as they went.

"Save me, Ivan the Poor!" begged Ivan the Rich. "I'll give you back your magic table-cloth and your goat."

"Two into the sack!" cried Ivan the Poor.

And at once the two cudgels crept into the sack and lay there quietly. And Ivan the Rich dragged himself to his house more dead than alive and came back again bringing the magic table-cloth and the goat that gave gold instead of milk.

From that day on Ivan the Poor and his family lived in good health and cheer and grew richer from year to year. And if you looked into their house today, you would see all the seven children sitting in a group and eating buckwheat porridge and cabbage soup. Their spoons are gaily coloured, their bowls are made of wood, there is butter in the porridge, and the soup is very good.

Fenist the Falcon

nce upon a time there lived a Peasant. His wife died and left him three daughters. The old man wanted to hire a servant-girl to help about the house, but his youngest daughter Máryushka said: "Don't hire a servant, Father, I shall keep house myself."

And so Máryushka began keeping house, and a fine house-keeper she made. There was nothing she could not do, and all she did she did well. Her father loved Máryushka dearly and was glad to have such a clever and hard-working daughter, and pretty too. For Máryushka was very beautiful! But as for her two sisters, they were ugly creatures, and full of envy and greed, and they were always painting and powdering their faces and dressing themselves in fancy clothes. They spent the days putting on new gowns and trying to look better than they were. But nothing ever pleased them long—neither gowns, nor shawls, nor high-heeled boots.

Now, one day the Peasant set out to market and he asked his daughters:

"What shall I buy for you, my dear daughters, what shall I bring that will please you?"

"Buy us each a shawl," said the two elder daughters. "And mind it has big flowers on it done in gold."

But Máryushka stood there and did not say a word.

Said the Peasant:

"And what would *you* like, Máryushka?"

"Buy me a feather of Fenist the Falcon, Father dear."

The Peasant went away, and in due time came back with the shawls. But he brought no feather, for he had not found one.

After a while he set out to market again.

"Well, little daughters, what shall I bring you?" asked he.

And the two elder daughters replied eagerly:

"Buy each of us a pair of silver-studded boots."

But Máryushka said again:

"Buy me a feather of Fenist the Falcon, Father dear."

All that day the Peasant walked about the market. He bought the boots, but could find no feather, and so came back without it.

Some time passed, and he set out to market for the third time, and his two elder daughters said:

"Buy us each a new gown."

But Máryushka said again:

"Buy me a feather of Fenist the Falcon, Father dear."

All that day the Peasant walked about the market, but no feather could he find. He drove out of town, and who should he meet on the way but a little old man.

"Good day, Grandfather!" said the Peasant.

"Good day to you, my good man. Where are you bound for?"

44

"Back to my village, Grandfather. And I'm that upset I don't know what to do. My youngest daughter asked me to buy her a feather of Fenist the Falcon, but I haven't found one."

"I have the feather you need; it is a charmed one, but I see you are a good man, so I think I'll let you have it."

And the little old man took out the feather and gave it to the Peasant. It looked just like any other feather, and as he rode home the Peasant wondered what good it could be to Máryushka.

He came home and gave the presents to his daughters. The two elder sisters tried on their new gowns and they laughed and laughed at Máryushka:

"Silly you were, and silly you will always be! Stick the feather in your hair—now won't you look fine with it!"

Máryushka made no answer, but she kept out of their way all that day. And when the whole house was asleep, she cast the feather on the floor and said softly:

"Come to me, Fenist the Falcon, my own love!"

And lo and behold! there appeared before her a youth so handsome as never was seen. Many hours did he spend with her, and in the morning struck the floor and turned into a falcon. Máryushka opened the window and the Falcon soared up into the blue sky.

For three nights she made him welcome. During the day he flew about in the blue heavens in the guise of a falcon; and when night fell he came back to Máryushka and turned into a handsome youth.

But on the fourth day Máryushka's two wicked sisters found out about them and went and told their father.

"You had better look to yourselves and leave your sister alone, my daughters," said he.

"Very well," thought they, "we shall see what comes further."

They stuck a row of sharp knives into the window-pane and then hid themselves and waited to see what would happen.

After a while the Bright Falcon appeared. He flew up to the window, but could not get into Máryushka's room. He fluttered about and beat against the pane till his whole breast was cut by the blades. But Máryushka slept and heard nothing.

Said the Falcon:

"If you need me you will find me, but it won't be easy. You shall not find me till you wear out three pairs of iron shoes, and break three iron staffs, and tear three iron caps."

Máryushka heard him and she sprang from bed and rushed to the window. But the Falcon was gone, and all that was left on the window were drops of his blood. Máryushka burst out crying and her tears washed off the drops of blood.

She went to her father and said:

"Do not scold me, Father, but let me go on my weary way. If I live, we shall meet again; if I die, then so must it be."

The Peasant was sorry to part with his favourite daughter, but he finally let her go.

So Máryushka went and ordered three pairs of iron shoes, three iron staffs, and three iron caps. And off she set on her long weary way to seek her heart's desire—Fenist the Falcon. Across open

46

fields she went, through dark forests and over tall mountains. The birds cheered her heart with merry songs, the brooks washed her white face, and the dark forests made her welcome. And no one could do harm to Máryushka, for all the wild beasts—grey wolves, brown bears and red foxes—would come flocking to her. On and on she went till at last one pair of her iron shoes wore out, one iron staff broke and one iron cap was torn.

Máryushka came to a glade in the woods and she saw a little hut on hen's feet spinning round and round.

"Little hut, little hut," said Máryushka, "turn your back to the trees and your face to me, please. Let me in to eat bread within."

The little hut turned its back to the trees and its face to Máryushka, and in Máryushka went. And whom did she see there but Baba-Yaga, the witch with the switch, a bony hag with a nose like a snag.

Baba-Yaga caught sight of Máryushka and muttered:

"Ugh, ugh, Russian blood, never met by me before, now I smell it at my door. Who comes here? Where from? Where to?"

"I am looking for Fenist the Falcon, Granny dear."

"He's a long way off, my pretty one! You will have to pass through the Thrice-Nine Lands to the Thrice-Ten Tsardom to find him. The Tsaritsa of the Thrice-Ten Tsardom is a wicked sorceress, and she gave him a potion to drink and while the spell was upon him, made him marry her. But I shall help you. Here, take this silver saucer and golden egg. When you come to the Thrice-Ten Tsardom, get yourself taken on as a servant-girl to the Tsaritsa. After the day's work is done, take the silver saucer and put the golden egg on it. It will start to roll about all by itself. Should they wish to buy it, do not sell it—ask them to let you see Fenist the Falcon."

Máryushka thanked Baba-Yaga and set out on her way. It grew dark in the forest, and she was too frightened to move, when all of a sudden she saw a Cat coming towards her. It sprang up to Máryushka and said, purring:

"Have no fear, Máryushka, it will be still worse farther on, but you must go on and never look back."

The Cat rubbed against her legs and was gone, and Máryushka went farther. The deeper she went into the forest the darker it grew. She walked on and on till her second pair of iron shoes wore out, her second iron staff broke and her second iron cap was torn, and she came to a little hut on hen's feet with a paling round it and glowing skulls on the pales.

Said Máryushka:

"Little hut, little hut, turn your back to the trees and your face to me, please. Let me in to eat bread within."

The little hut turned its back to the trees and its face to Máryushka, and Máryushka went in. And there sat Baba-Yaga, the witch with the switch, a bony hag with a nose like a snag.

Baba-Yaga caught sight of Máryushka and muttered:

"Ugh, ugh, Russian blood, never met by me before, now I smell it at my door. Who comes here? Where from? Where to?"

"I am seeking Fenist the Falcon, Granny."

"And have you been to my sister's?"

"Yes, Granny dear, I have."

"Very well then, my beauty, I will help you. Take this golden needle and silver frame. The needle works all by itself and embroiders red velvet with silver and gold. Should they wish to buy it, do not sell it—ask them to let you see Fenist the Falcon."

Máryushka thanked Baba-Yaga and went on her way. There came a crashing and a thundering and a whistling in the forest, and the skulls crowning the pales shone with a weird light. Máryushka was terrified. She looked, and lo! a Dog came running up to her.

"Bow-wow, Máryushka, have no fear, my dear, it will be still worse, but you must go on and never look back."

So it spoke and was gone. Máryushka walked farther, and the forest grew darker, and its trees and shrubs scratched her knees and caught at her sleeves. But she went on and on and never looked back.

Whether she walked for a long or a little time nobody knows, but at last the third pair of iron shoes wore out, the third iron staff broke and the third iron cap was torn. Máryushka came to a glade in the forest and she saw a little hut on hen's feet with a paling all round and glowing horse skulls on the pales.

Said Máryushka:

"Little hut, little hut, turn your back to the trees and your face to me, please."

The hut turned its back to the trees and its face to Máryushka, and Máryushka went in. And there sat Baba-Yaga, the witch with the switch, a bony hag with a nose like a snag.

Baba-Yaga saw Máryushka and muttered:

"Ugh, ugh, Russian blood,

never met by me before, now I smell it at my door. Who comes here? Where from? Where to?"

"I'm looking for Fenist the Falcon, Granny!"

"It is no easy task to find him, my beauty, but I shall help you. Here, take this silver distaff and this golden spindle. Hold the spindle in your hands and it will spin all by itself and the thread will come out all gold."

"Thank you, Granny."

"Save your thanks until afterwards, and now listen to me. Should they wish to buy the golden spindle, don't sell it, but ask them to let you see Fenist the Falcon."

Máryushka thanked Baba-Yaga and went on her way. And in the forest there came a roaring and a rumbling and a whistling. The owls spun and wheeled round and round and the mice crawled out of their holes and rushed straight at Máryushka. She looked, and lo! a Grey Wolf came running up to her.

Said the Wolf:

"Have no fear, Máryushka. Get on my back and never look behind you."

Máryushka climbed on the Wolf's back and off they went in a flash. They passed wide steppes and velvet meadows, they crossed honey rivers with jelly banks and they climbed tall mountains that touched the clouds. On and on raced the Wolf with Máryushka on his back and he reached a crystal palace with a carved porch and windows. And there was the Tsaritsa herself looking out of a window.

"Here we are, Máryushka," said the Wolf. "Climb off my back and go and ask to be taken on as a servant-girl at the palace."

Máryushka sprang down to the ground, took her bundle and, thanking the Wolf, went to the palace. She walked up to the Tsaritsa, bowed and said:

"I beg your pardon, I don't know your name, but do you need a servant-girl?"

"Yes, I do," the Tsaritsa replied. "I have long been looking for one. But she must be able to spin, to weave and to embroider."

"I can do all that," said Máryushka.

"Come in then and set to work."

And so Máryushka became a servant-girl. She worked all day,

and when night came she took
out her golden egg and silver
saucer and said:

"Roll, roll, golden egg, over
the silver saucer, and show me
my Fenist, my own love."

And the golden egg rolled
over the silver saucer, and there
upon it Fenist the Falcon appeared. Máryushka gazed at
him and her tears ran fast.

"Fenist, my Fenist, why have
you left poor me to shed tears
without you?"

The Tsaritsa overheard her
and said:

"Sell me your silver saucer
and golden egg, Máryushka."

"No," replied Máryushka,
"they are not for sale, but you
may have them free if you let
me see Fenist the Falcon."

The Tsaritsa thought for a
while and then she said:

"Very well, let it be so. Tonight, when he falls asleep, I
will let you see him."

Night came, and Máryushka
went to his chamber and saw
Fenist the Falcon. Her love
lay fast asleep and could not

be wakened. She looked and looked and could not have enough of looking, and she kissed him on his sugar-sweet mouth and clung to him, but he slept on and did not wake. Morning set in, but still Máryushka could not rouse her beloved.

All that day she worked and in the evening took out her silver frame and golden needle. She sat there and sewed and said over again:

"Get embroidered, little towel, get embroidered, let my Fenist the Falcon have something to wipe his face with in the morning."

The Tsaritsa overheard her and said:

"Sell me your silver frame and golden needle, Máryushka."

"No, that I cannot do," Máryushka replied, "but you may have them free if you let me see Fenist the Falcon."

The Tsaritsa thought for a while and then she said:

"Very well, let it be so. You can come to see him tonight."

Night came, and Máryushka went to his chamber and saw Fenist the Falcon lying there fast asleep.

"O my Fenist, my brave and handsome Falcon, arise, wake up!" she said.

But Fenist slept on as fast as ever, and Máryushka could not wake him, try as she might.

At daybreak Máryushka set to work, and she took out her silver distaff and golden spindle. And the Tsaritsa saw her and began begging her to sell them. But Máryushka said:

"No, they are not for sale, but you may have them for nothing if only you let me see Fenist the Falcon."

"Very well," said the other, and she thought to herself: "She won't wake him anyway."

Night drew on, and Máryushka went to his chamber, but Fenist lay there as fast asleep as ever.

"O my Fenist, my brave and handsome Falcon, arise, wake up!" she said.

But Fenist slept on and did not wake.

Máryushka tried over and over again to wake him, but she could not. And it would soon be morning. She burst into tears and said:

"Fenist, dear Fenist, my own love, arise and open your eyes, look at your Máryushka, press her close to your heart!"

And Máryushka's hot tear fell on to Fenist's bare shoulder and burnt it. Fenist the Falcon stirred and he opened his eyes and saw Máryushka. He took her in his arms and kissed her.

"Can it be you, my Máryushka? So you have worn out three pairs of iron shoes and broken three iron staffs and torn three iron caps? Cry no more. Let us go home now."

They began getting ready for the homeward journey, but the Tsaritsa saw them and bade her trumpeters spread the news of her husband's faithlessness throughout the land.

And the princes and merchants of her land came together to hold council and decide how to punish Fenist the Falcon.

And Fenist the Falcon stood up and said:

"Which do you think is the true wife, she who loves me with all her heart or she who sells and betrays me?"

And everyone had to agree that his true wife was Máryushka.

After that they went back to their own land. They held a feast there, and so grand was it that it is remembered to this day, and all the guns were fired and all the trumpets blew at their wedding. And from that day on they lived in love and cheer and grew richer from year to year.

Sister Alyonushka
and Brother Ivanushka

nce there lived an old man and his wife, and they had a daughter named Alyonushka and a son named Ivanushka.

The old man and the old woman died, and Alyonushka and Ivanushka were left all alone in the world.

Alyonushka set off to work and took her little brother with her. They had a long way to go, and a wide field to cross, and after they had been walking for a time, Ivanushka began to feel very thirsty.

"Sister Alyonushka, I am thirsty," he said.

"Be patient, little brother, we shall soon come to a well."

They walked and they walked, and the sun was now high up in the sky, and so hot were the two that they felt very blue. They came upon a cow's hoof filled with water, and Ivanushka said:

"May I drink out of the hoof, Sister Alyonushka?"

"No, little brother. If you do, you will turn into a calf."

Ivanushka obeyed, and they walked on a bit farther.

The sun was still high up in the sky, and the heat was so bad that they felt very sad. They came upon a horse's hoof filled with water, and Ivanushka said:

"May I drink out of the hoof, Sister Alyonushka?"

"No, little brother. If you do, you will turn into a foal."

Ivanushka sighed and they walked on again.

They walked and they walked, but the sun was still high up in the sky, and the air was so dry that they felt they could die. They came upon a goat's hoof filled with water, and Ivanushka said:

"I am dying of thirst, Sister Alyonushka. May I drink out of the hoof?"

"No, little brother. If you do, you will turn into a kid."

But Ivanushka did not heed his sister and drank out of the goat's hoof.

And the moment he did so he turned into a little white goat. Alyonushka called her brother, and instead of Ivanushka the goat came running up to her.

Alyonushka burst into tears. She sat sobbing on the ground by a stack of hay while the little goat skipped round in play.

Just then a Merchant chanced to be riding by.

"What are you crying for, pretty maid?" asked he.

Alyonushka told him of her trouble.

Said the Merchant:

"Marry me, pretty maid. I will dress you in gold and silver, and the little goat will live with us."

Alyonushka thought it over and agreed to marry the Merchant.

They lived together happily, and the little goat lived with them and ate and drank with Alyonushka out of the same cup.

One day the Merchant went away from home and all of a sudden a Witch appeared out of nowhere. She stood under Alyonushka's window and begged her ever so sweetly to go and bathe in the river with her.

Alyonushka followed the Witch to the river, and when they got there the Witch fell upon Alyonushka and, tying a stone round her neck, threw her into the water and herself took on her shape.

Then she put on Alyonushka's clothes and went to her house, and no one guessed she was not Alyonushka but a Witch. The Merchant came home, and even he did not guess.

Only the little goat knew what had happened. He went about with drooping head and did not touch food or drink. Morning and evening he never left the river bank and, standing at the water's edge, called:

"Sister, dear Sister Alyonushka! Swim out, swim out to me."

The Witch learned of this, and she asked her husband to kill the little goat.

The Merchant was sorry for the little goat, for he had become very fond of him. But the Witch kept coaxing and wheedling so that there was nothing to be done, and he gave in at last.

"All right, you kill him then," he said.

The Witch had big fires kindled, big pots heated and big knives sharpened.

The little goat found out that he was going to be killed, so he said to the Merchant:

"Let me go to the river before I die and have a last little drink."

"Go," said the Merchant.

The little goat ran to the river, stood on the bank and cried piteously:

> *"Sister, dear Sister Alyonushka!*
> *Swim out, swim out to me.*
> *Fires are burning high,*
> *Pots are boiling,*
> *Knives are ringing,*
> *And I am going to die."*

And Alyonushka answered from out the river:

> *"Brother, dear Brother Ivanushka!*
> *A heavy stone lies on my shoulders,*
> *Silken weeds entangle my legs,*
> *Yellow sands press hard on my breast.'*

The Witch set out in search of the goat, but she could not find him, so she called a servant and said:

"Go and find the goat and bring him to me."

The servant went to the river, and what did he see but the little goat running up and down the bank, calling piteously:

> *"Sister, dear Sister Alyonushka!*
> *Swim out, swim out to me.*
> *Fires are burning high,*
> *Pots are boiling,*
> *Knives are ringing,*
> *And I am going to die."*

And from the river someone's voice called back:

"Brother, dear Brother Ivanushka!
A heavy stone lies on my shoulders,
Silken weeds entangle my legs,
Yellow sands press hard on my breast."

The servant ran home and told his master what he had heard and seen. The Merchant called some people together, they went down to the river and, casting a silken net, dragged Alyonushka out on to the bank. They untied the stone which was round her neck, dipped her in spring water and dressed her in bright clothes. And Alyonushka came back to life and was more beautiful than ever.

The little goat was wild with joy, he turned three somersaults, and lo and behold! He was changed into his proper shape again.

And the wicked Witch was tied to a horse's tail and the horse turned loose in an open field.

Chestnut-Grey

Once upon a time there lived an old man who had three sons. The two elder sons were well-favoured young men who liked to wear fine clothes and were thrifty husbandmen, but the youngest, Ivan the Fool, was none of those things. He spent most of his time at home sitting on the stove ledge and only going out to gather mushrooms in the forest.

When the time came for the old man to die, he called his three sons to his side and said to them:

"When I die, you must come to my grave every night for three nights and bring me some bread to eat."

The old man died and was buried, and that night the time came for the eldest brother to go to his grave. But he was too lazy or else too frightened to go, and he said to Ivan the Fool:

"If you will only go in my stead to our father's grave tonight, Ivan, I shall buy you a honey-cake."

Ivan readily agreed, took some bread and went to his father's grave. He sat down by the grave and waited to see what would happen. On the stroke of midnight the earth crumbled apart and the old father rose out of his grave and said:

"Who is there? Is it you, my first-born? Tell me how everything fares in Rus: are the dogs barking, the wolves howling or my child weeping?"

And Ivan replied:

"It is I, your son, Father. And all is quiet in Rus."

Then the father ate his fill of the bread Ivan had brought and lay down in his grave again. As for Ivan, he went home, stopping to gather some mushrooms on the way.

When he reached home, his eldest brother asked:

"Did you see our father?"

"Yes, I did," Ivan replied.

"Did he eat of the bread you brought?"

"Yes. He ate till he could eat no more."

Another day passed by, and it was the second brother's turn to go to the grave. But he was too lazy or else too frightened to go, and he said to Ivan:

"If only you go in my stead, Ivan, I shall make you a pair of bast shoes."

"Very well," said Ivan, "I shall go."

He took some bread, went to his father's grave and sat there waiting. On the stroke of midnight the earth crumbled apart and the old father rose out of the grave and said:

"Who is there? Is it you, my second-born? Tell me how everything fares in Rus: are the dogs barking, the wolves howling or my child weeping?"

And Ivan replied:

"It is I, your son, Father. And all is quiet in Rus."

Then the father ate his fill of the bread Ivan had brought and lay down in his grave again. And Ivan went home, stopping to gather some mushrooms on the way. He reached home and his second brother asked him:

"Did our father eat of the bread you brought?"

"Yes," Ivan replied. "He ate till he could eat no more."

On the third night it was Ivan's turn to go to the grave and he said to his brothers:

"For two nights I have gone to our father's grave. Now it is your turn to go and I will stay home and rest."

"Oh, no," the brothers replied. "You must go again, Ivan, for you are used to it."

"Very well," Ivan agreed, "I shall go."

He took some bread and went to the grave, and on the stroke of midnight the earth crumbled apart and the old father rose out of the grave.

"Who is there?" said he. "Is it you, Ivan, my third-born? Tell me how everything fares in Rus: are the dogs barking, the wolves howling or my child weeping?"

And Ivan replied:

"It is I, your son Ivan, Father. And all is quiet in Rus."

The father ate his fill of the bread Ivan had brought and said to him:

"You were the only one to obey my command, Ivan. You were not afraid to come to my grave for three nights. Now you must go out into the open field and shout: 'Chestnut-Grey, hear and obey! I call thee nigh to do or die!' When the horse appears before you, climb into his right ear and come out of his left, and you will turn into as comely a lad as ever was seen. Then mount the horse and go where you will."

Ivan took the bridle his father gave him, thanked him and went home, stopping to gather some mushrooms on the way. He reached home and his brothers asked him:

"Did you see our father, Ivan?"

"Yes, I did," Ivan replied.

"Did he eat of the bread you brought?"

"Yes, he ate till he could eat no more and he bade me not to go to his grave any more."

Now, at this very time the Tsar had a call sounded abroad for all handsome, unmarried young men to gather at court. The Tsar's daughter, Tsarevna Lovely, had ordered a castle of twelve pillars and twelve rows of oak logs to be built for herself. And there she meant to sit at the window of the top chamber and await the one who would leap on his steed as high as her window and place a kiss on her lips. To him who succeeded, whether of high or of low birth,

the Tsar would give Tsarevna Lovely, his daughter, in marriage and half his tsardom besides.

News of this came to the ears of Ivan's brothers, who agreed between them to try their luck.

They gave a feed of oats to their goodly steeds and led them from the stables, and themselves put on their best apparel and combed down their curly locks. And Ivan, who was sitting on the stove ledge behind the chimney, said to them:

"Take me with you, my brothers, and let me try my luck, too."

"You silly sit-on-the-stove!" laughed they. "You will only be mocked at if you go with us. Better go and hunt for mushrooms in the forest."

The brothers mounted their goodly steeds, cocked their hats, gave a whistle and a whoop and galloped off down the road in a cloud of dust. And Ivan took the bridle his father had given him, went out into the open field and shouted as his father had told him:

"Chestnut-Grey, hear and obey! I call thee nigh to do or die!"

And, lo and behold! a charger came running towards him. The earth shook under his hoofs, his nostrils spurted flame, and clouds of smoke poured from his ears. The charger galloped up to Ivan, stood stock-still and said:

"What is your wish, Ivan?"

Ivan stroked the steed's neck, bridled him, climbed into his right ear and came out through his left. And lo! he was turned into a youth as fair as the sky at dawn, the handsomest youth that ever was born. He got up on Chestnut-Grey's back and set off for the Tsar's palace. On went Chestnut-Grey with a snort and a neigh, passing mountain and dale with a swish of his tail, skirting houses and trees as quick as the breeze.

When Ivan arrived at court, the palace grounds were teeming with people. There stood the castle of twelve pillars and twelve rows of oak logs, and in its highest attic, at the window of her chamber, sat Tsarevna Lovely.

The Tsar stepped out on the porch and said:

"He from amongst you, good youths, who leaps up on his steed as high as yon window and places a kiss upon my daughter's lips, shall have her in marriage and half my tsardom besides."

One after another the wooers of Tsarevna Lovely rode up and pranced and leaped, but, alas, the window was out of their reach. Ivan's two brothers tried with the rest, but with no better success.

When Ivan's turn came, he sent Chestnut-Grey at a gallop and with a whoop and a shout leapt up as high as the highest row of logs but two. On he came again and leapt up as high as the highest row but one. One more chance was left him, and he pranced and whirled Chestnut-Grey round and round till the steed chafed and fumed. Then, bounding like fire past her window, he took a great leap and placed a kiss on the honey-sweet lips of Tsarevna Lovely. And the Tsarevna struck his brow with her signet-ring and left her seal on him.

The people roared: "Hold him! Stop him!" but Ivan and his steed were gone in a cloud of dust.

Off they galloped to the open field, and Ivan climbed into Chestnut-Grey's left ear and came out through his right, and lo!

he was changed to his proper shape again. Then he let Chestnut-Grey run free and himself went home, stopping to gather some mushrooms on the way. He came into the house, bound his forehead with a rag, climbed up on the stove ledge and lay there as before.

By and by his brothers arrived and began telling him where they had been and what they had seen.

"Many were the wooers of the Tsarevna, and handsome, too," they said. "But one there was who outshone them all. He leapt up on his fiery steed to the Tsarevna's window and he kissed her lips. We saw him come, but we did not see him go."

Said Ivan from his perch behind the chimney:

"Perhaps it was me you saw."

His brothers flew into a temper and said:

"Stop your silly talk, fool! Sit there on your stove and eat your mushrooms."

Then Ivan untied the rag that covered the seal from the Tsar-

70

evna's signet-ring and at once a bright glow lit up the hut. The brothers were frightened and cried:

"What are you doing, fool? You'll burn down the house!"

The next day the Tsar held a feast to which he summoned all his subjects, boyars and nobles and common folk, rich and poor, young and old.

Ivan's brothers, too, prepared to attend the feast.

"Take me with you, my brothers," Ivan begged.

"What?" they laughed. "You will only be mocked at by all. Stay here on your stove and eat your mushrooms."

The brothers then mounted their goodly steeds and rode away, and Ivan followed them on foot. He came to the Tsar's palace and seated himself in a far corner. Tsarevna Lovely now began to make the round of all the guests. She offered each a drink from the cup of mead she carried and she looked at their brows to see if her seal were there.

She made the round of all the guests except Ivan, and when she approached him her heart sank. He was all smutted with soot and his hair stood on end.

Said Tsarevna Lovely:

"Who are you? Where do you come from? And why is your brow bound with a rag?"

"I hurt myself in falling," Ivan replied.

The Tsarevna unwound the rag and a bright glow at once lit up the palace.

"That is my seal!" she cried. "Here is my betrothed!"

The Tsar came up to Ivan, looked at him and said:

"Oh, no, Tsarevna Lovely! This cannot be your betrothed! He is all sooty and very plain."

Said Ivan to the Tsar:

"Allow me to wash my face, Tsar."

The Tsar gave him leave to do so, and Ivan came out into the courtyard and shouted as his father had taught him to:

"Chestnut-Grey, hear and obey! I call thee nigh to do or die!"

And lo and behold! Chestnut-Grey came galloping towards him. The earth shook under his hoofs, his nostrils spurted flame, and clouds of smoke poured from his ears. Ivan climbed into his right ear and came out through his left and was turned into a youth as fair as the sky at dawn, the handsomest youth that ever was born. All the people in the palace gave a great gasp when they saw him.

No words were wasted after that.

Ivan married Tsarevna Lovely, and a merry feast was held to celebrate their wedding.

Father Frost

Once upon a time there lived an old man with his second wife, and they each had a daughter. He had a daughter and so had she.

Everyone knows what stepmothers are like. If you do wrong, you get a beating, and if you do right, you get a beating all the same. Not so with the stepmother's own daughter: she is petted and praised for a good and clever lass no matter what she does.

The old man's daughter rose before daybreak to look after the cattle, bring firewood and water into the house, light the stove and sweep the floor. But her stepmother found fault with everything and fussed and scolded her all day long.

A wind howls loud and then it drops. But there is no quieting an old dame once she is roused. The stepmother made up her mind to do her stepdaughter to death.

"Take her away, old one," she said to her husband, "I can't bear the sight of her. Take her to the forest into the biting frost and leave her there."

The old man wept and sorrowed but he knew he could do nothing, for his wife always had her way. So he harnessed his horse and called to his daughter:

74

"Come, my sweet child, get into the sledge."

He took the homeless girl to the forest, dumped her into a snow-drift beneath a large fir-tree and drove away.

It was very cold, and the girl sat under the fir-tree and shivered. Suddenly she heard Father Frost near by leaping from tree to tree and crackling and snapping among the twigs. In a twinkling he was on the top of the very tree beneath which she sat.

"Are you warm, my lass?" he called.

"Yes, I'm very warm, Father Frost!" she answered.

Father Frost came down lower and he crackled and snapped louder than ever.

"Are you warm, my lass?" he called again. "Are you warm, my pretty one?"

The girl was scarcely able to fetch her breath, but she said:

"Yes, I'm very warm, Father Frost!"

Father Frost came down still lower, crackling and snapping very loud indeed.

"Are you warm, my lass?" he asked. "Are you warm, my pretty one? Are you warm, my sweet one?"

The girl was growing numb and could hardly move her tongue, but still she said:

"I'm very warm, good Father Frost!"

And Father Frost took pity on the girl and he wrapped her up in his fluffy furs and downy quilts.

Meanwhile, the stepmother was baking pancakes and preparing for the funeral feast. Said she to her husband:

"Go to the forest, you old croaker, and bring back your daughter to be buried!"

The old man went to the forest and there, in the very spot where he had left her, sat his daughter, very gay and rosy. She was wrapped in a sable coat and clad in silver and gold. Beside her stood a large basket full of costly presents.

The old man was overjoyed. He seated his daughter in the sledge, put the basket in beside her and drove home.

Now the old woman was still baking the pancakes when suddenly she heard her little dog under the table saying:

"Bow-wow! The old man's daughter comes a rich bride and fair,
But the old woman's daughter, she will marry ne'er!"

The old woman threw a pancake to the dog and said:
"You speak wrong, dog! You must say:

'The old woman's daughter will be wooed and won,
But the old man's daughter is dead and gone!'"

The dog ate the pancake, but still it said:

"Bow-wow! The old man's daughter comes a rich bride and fair,
But the old woman's daughter, she will marry ne'er!"

The old woman threw more pancakes to the dog and when this did not help she beat it, but still the dog said just what it had before.

All of a sudden the gate creaked, the door opened and in walked the old man's daughter, dazzling in her attire of silver and gold.

Behind her came her father carrying a large and heavy basket full of costly gifts. The old woman looked and her hands dropped.

"Harness the horse, you old croaker!" said she to her husband. "Take my daughter to the forest and leave her in the same place as yours."

The old man put the old woman's daughter in the sledge, took her to the forest to the same place, dumped her into the snowdrift underneath the tall fir-tree and drove away.

There sat the old woman's daughter and she was so cold her teetn chattered.

By and by Father Frost came leaping from tree to tree, crackling and snapping among the twigs and stopping now and then to glance at the old woman's daughter.

"Are you warm, my lass?" he called.

Said she in reply:

"Oh, no, I'm terribly cold! Don't scrunch and crackle so, Frost!"

Father Frost came down lower, and he crackled and snapped the louder.

"Are you warm, my lass?" he called. "Are you warm, my pretty one?"

"Oh, no," said she, "I'm numb all over! Go away, Frost!"

But Father Frost came down still lower and he crackled and snapped ever louder and his breath grew colder and colder.

"Are you warm, my lass?" he called again. "Are you warm, my pretty one?"

"Oh, no!" she cried. "I'm frozen! A plague on you, you old Frost! I hope the earth swallows you!"

Father Frost was so angered by these words that he gripped her with all his might and froze the old woman's daughter to death.

Day had barely dawned when the old woman said to her husband: "Make haste and harness the horse, you old croaker. Go fetch my daughter and bring her back clad in silver and gold."

The old man drove away and the little dog under the table said:

> *"Bow-wow! The old man's daughter will soon be wed,
> But the old woman's daughter is cold and dead!"*

The old woman threw the dog a pie and said: "You speak wrong, dog! You must say:

> *'The old woman's daughter comes a rich bride and fair,
> But the old man's daughter, she will marry ne'er!'"*

But the dog said just what it had before:

> *"Bow-wow! The old woman's daughter is cold and dead!"*

Just then the gate creaked and the old woman rushed out to meet her daughter. She turned back the bast cover and there lay her daughter in the sledge, dead.

The old woman broke out into loud weeping, but it was all too late.

Go I Know Not Where, Fetch I Know Not What

In a certain tsardom there was a Tsar. He was a single man, unmarried, and he had in his service an Archer named Andrei.

One day the Archer went out hunting. He tramped about the woods all day long, but no game came his way. It was getting late, so feeling weary and out of humour, he turned his way homewards. Suddenly he saw a turtle-dove sitting in a tree.

"I may as well have a shot at it," thought he.

So he shot and winged the dove, and it dropped from the tree on to the damp earth. Andrei picked it up and was about to wring its neck and put it in his pouch, when the bird spoke to him in a human voice and said:

"Do not kill me, Archer Andrei, do not wring my poor neck. Take me home alive and put me in the window. But mind, as soon as I begin to doze, slap me with your right hand, and great good fortune shall be yours."

Andrei the Archer could not believe his ears.

"What is this?" he thought. "The bird looks just like any other bird, yet it speaks in a human voice."

He took the dove home, put it in the window and waited.

By and by the dove tucked its head under its wing and dozed off, and Andrei, never forgetting what it had told him, slapped it with his right hand. The dove fell on the floor and turned into Tsarevna Maria, a maiden as fair as the sky at dawn, the fairest maiden that ever was born.

Said Tsarevna Maria to the Archer:

"You have managed to catch me, now manage to keep me. Happy is the wooing that is not long a-doing. Marry me and I will make you a faithful and cheerful wife."

And so the matter was settled. Andrei the Archer married Tsarevna Maria, and he and his young wife were very happy together. But he did not neglect his duties. Every morning before daybreak he would go to the forest, shoot wild fowl and take them to the Tsar's kitchen. And thus it went on for a time, till one day Tsarevna Maria said:

"You and I are much too poor, Andrei."

"I'm afraid we are."

"If you borrow a hundred rubles and buy me silks with it, I shall see that our life is bettered."

Andrei did as she had told him. He went to his friends, borrowed a ruble here, two there, and bought silks with the money. He brought the silks to his wife, and she took them and said:

"Now go to bed; night is the mother of counsel."

Andrei went to bed, and Tsarevna Maria sat down to weave. All night long she wove, and she made a rug the like of which the world had never seen. On it was pictured the whole tsardom, with all its towns and villages, its woods and fields, the birds in the sky, the beasts in the woods, the fish in the seas, and the moon and sun shining down upon it all.

In the morning Tsarevna Maria gave her husband the rug and said:

"Take it to Merchants' Row and sell it, but mind do not name your own price. Take whatever they give you."

Andrei took the rug, hung it over his arm and went to Merchants' Row.

Presently a merchant ran up to him and said:

"How much do you want for the rug, my good man?"

"You are a merchant, name your own price."

The merchant thought and thought, but he could not price the rug. Then another came up, and after him another and still another. Soon there was a whole crowd of them. They all looked at the rug and marvelled, but none could price it.

Just then the Tsar's Councillor came riding by, and he wondered what all the to-do was about. He got out of his carriage, elbowed his way through the crowd and said:

"Greetings, merchants, from far lands and near. What is going on here?"

"We cannot price this rug," they said.

The Tsar's Councillor looked at the rug and was struck with wonder.

"Now tell me the truth, Archer, where did you get this marvellous rug?" he asked.

"My wife made it," said the Archer.

"And how much do you want for it?"

"I do not know. My wife said I was to take whatever I was given."

"Then here's ten thousand rubles, Archer."

Andrei took the money, handed over the rug and went home. And the Tsar's Councillor rode to the palace and showed the rug to the Tsar.

The Tsar looked, and he marvelled, for there was his whole tsardom before his eyes. It fairly took his breath away!

"Say what you like, but I shall not give you back this rug," said he.

He got out twenty thousand rubles and gave them to his Councillor, and the Councillor took the money and thought:

"It does not matter, I shall have another, still better, made for myself."

He got into his carriage again and rode to the outskirts of the town. He found the hut in which Andrei the Archer lived and knocked at the door. Tsarevna Maria opened it, and the Tsar's Councillor put one foot over the threshold, but his other remained rooted to the ground. He lost his tongue and forgot what he had come for. There before him stood a woman so beautiful that he could have feasted his eyes on her for ever.

Tsarevna Maria waited for him to speak, and when he did not, she pushed him out and shut the door on him. After a while he collected his wits and betook himself home. But from that day on he could neither eat nor drink for thinking of the Archer's wife.

The Tsar saw the man was not himself and asked him what was wrong. Said the Councillor:

"Ah, Your Majesty, I have seen the Archer's wife and I cannot get her out of my mind. She has bewitched me, really and truly, and I can do nothing to break the spell."

Now this made the Tsar eager to take a look at the Archer's wife. He put on common clothes, went to the outskirts of the town, found the hut in which Andrei the Archer lived and knocked at the door. Tsarevna Maria opened it, and the Tsar put one foot over the threshold, but his other foot remained rooted to the ground. There he stood, and he was dumb with wonder for never had he seen anyone so beautiful!

Tsarevna Maria waited for the Tsar to speak, and when he did not, she pushed him out and shut the door on him.

The Tsar was badly smitten.

"Why should I live alone?" thought he. "Here is a lovely bride for me. She was meant to be a Tsar's wife, not an Archer's."

The Tsar went back to his palace, and a wicked plan took shape in his head: to steal his wife from a living husband. He sent for his Councillor and said:

84

"Think of a way to get rid of Andrei the Archer. I want to marry his wife. If you help me, I shall reward you with towns and villages and gold, but if you do not, I shall cut your head off."

The Tsar's Councillor was sorely troubled. He could think of no way to get rid of the Archer, and so, looking sad and downcast, he went to a tavern to drown his sorrow in wine.

A tavern frequenter in a ragged *caftan* came up to him and said:

"Why do you look so sad, Tsar's Councillor? What is it that troubles you?"

"Be off with you, ragamuffin!"

"Better buy me a drink and I will give you some good advice."

The Tsar's Councillor gave him a glass of wine and told him his trouble.

"Andrei the Archer is a simple fellow," said the ragamuffin. "It would be easy to get rid of him if his wife were not so clever. We must think of something that will baffle even her. I believe I know what will. Go back and tell the Tsar to send Andrei the Archer to the Next World to find out how his dead father, the old Tsar, is doing. Andrei will go and never come back."

The Tsar's Councillor thanked the ragamuffin and ran back to the Tsar.

"I have thought of a way to get rid of the Archer," said he, and he told the Tsar what to do.

The Tsar was greatly pleased and sent at once for Andrei the Archer.

"Well, Andrei," he said, "you have served me faithfully, but there is one more service I must ask of you. Go to the Next World and find out how my father is doing. If you do not, I'll out with my sword and off with your head."

Andrei went home. He sat down on the bench and he hung his head.

"Why are you so sad, Andrei?" asked Tsarevna María.

Andrei told her what the Tsar wanted him to do.

"What a thing to worry about!" said Tsarevna María. "A trifling task; the real task is yet to come. Go to bed; night is the mother of counsel."

On the following morning, as soon as Andrei woke up, Tsarevna María gave him a bag of biscuits and a gold ring.

"Go to the Tsar and ask him to let you take the Councillor with you, so that he will know you have really been to the Next World. When you set forth with your way-companion, throw the ring in front of you and it will show you the way."

Andrei took the bag of biscuits and the ring, said good-bye to his wife and went to ask the Tsar to send his Councillor with him. The Tsar could not very well refuse, and he ordered the Councillor to go with Andrei. The two started out together, Andrei threw down the ring and off it rolled. He followed it through open fields and mossy marshes, across lakes and rivers, and behind him trudged the Tsar's Councillor. Whenever they grew tired of walking, they would eat some biscuits and then set off again.

Whether they walked for a long or a little time nobody knows, but by and by they came to a great, thick forest. They climbed down a deep ravine, and there the ring stopped.

Andrei and the Tsar's Councillor sat down to eat some biscuits. And who should they see but a doddering old Tsar pulling a cart of firewood, and a great big load it was, too, while two devils, one on his right, the other on his left, drove him on with cudgels.

"Look yonder," said Andrei. "Isn't that the Tsar's dead father?"

"It is indeed," said the Councillor.

"Hi, gentlemen!" shouted Andrei to the devils. "Let that old sinner go for a minute, I should like to have a word with him."

"Do you think we have time to stand about and wait?" replied the devils. "Or do you expect us to draw the wood ourselves?"

"I have a man here who can take his place," said Andrei.

So the devils unhitched the old Tsar and hitched the Councillor to the cart instead. They struck him with their cudgels, one on the left side, the other on the right, and the Councillor bent double but pulled as best he could.

Andrei asked the old Tsar how life was treating him.

"Ah, Archer Andrei," said the Tsar, "I am having a bad time of it in the Next World. Remember me to my son and tell him not to ill-treat people, or else he too will have a bad time of it when he gets here."

They had scarcely finished talking when the devils came back with the empty cart. Andrei took his leave of the old Tsar, the Councillor rejoined him, and they set out for home.

By and by they came to their own tsardom and went to the palace. The Tsar saw the Archer and he flew at him in a rage.

"How dare you come back!" he cried.

"I have seen your dead father in the Next World. He's having a bad time there," said the Archer. "He sends you his best wishes and says you are not to ill-treat people if you do not want to have as bad a time of it as he has."

"And how are you going to prove you have been to the Next World and seen my father?"

"I can prove it by the marks the devils' cudgels left on your Councillor's back."

That was proof enough, so the Tsar had to let Andrei go—what else could he do?

Said he to his Councillor:

"If you do not think of a way to get rid of the Archer, then I'll out with my sword and off with your head."

The Councillor was more troubled than ever. He went to the tavern, sat down at a table and called for wine. Just then the selfsame ragamuffin came up to him and said:

"What makes you so sad, Tsar's Councillor? What is it that troubles you? Buy me a drink and I will give you some good advice."

The Councillor gave him a glass of wine and told him his trouble.

"Do not worry," said the ragamuffin. "Go back and tell the Tsar to have the Archer do him this service—a thing hard to think of, let alone to do: he is to go beyond the Thrice-Nine Lands to the Thrice-Ten Tsardom and fetch Croon-Cat."

The Councillor ran off to the Tsar and told him how to get rid of the Archer. The Tsar sent for Andrei.

"Well, Andrei, you have done me one service, now do me another," said he. "Go beyond the Thrice-Nine Lands to the Thrice-Ten Tsardom and bring me Croon-Cat. If you do not, I'll out with my sword and off with your head."

Andrei went home with drooping head and told his wife what task the Tsar had set him.

"What a thing to worry about!" said Tsarevna Maria. "A trifling task; the real task is yet to come. Go to bed; night is the mother of counsel."

89

Andrei went to bed, and Tsarevna Maria went to the smithy and told the blacksmiths to forge three iron caps, a pair of iron tongs and three rods—one of iron, another of copper, and the third of tin.

Early next morning Tsarevna Maria woke Andrei up.

"Here are three caps, a pair of tongs and three rods—go beyond the Thrice-Nine Lands to the Thrice-Ten Tsardom. Three *versts* short of it, you will feel very sleepy—that will be Croon-Cat casting her spell over you. But mind you don't fall asleep. Fold your hands, drag your feet, and if need be, roll along the ground. If you fall asleep, Croon-Cat will kill you."

And telling him just what to do and how to do it, Tsarevna Maria saw him off on his errand.

The tale is short in telling, but the deed is long in doing. Andrei the Archer came at last to the Thrice-Ten Tsardom, and three *versts* short of it he began to feel sleepy. He put the three iron caps on his head, folded his hands, dragged his feet, and when nothing else helped, rolled along the ground.

Somehow he managed to keep awake and found himself at a tall post.

When Croon-Cat saw Andrei she growled and snarled and jumped off the post straight on to his head. She broke the first cap, she broke the second, and was going for the third when Andrei caught her with the tongs, dragged her down to the ground and fell to trouncing her with the rods. First he whipped her with the iron rod; when the iron rod broke he flogged her with the copper rod; and when the copper rod broke he laid about him with the tin one.

The tin rod bent but did not break—it only curled round her body. As Andrei flogged her Croon-Cat told him fairy-tales about priests, about deacons, and about priests' daughters. But Andrei turned a deaf ear and flogged away with might and main.

90

That was more than Croon-Cat could stand, and, seeing that her evil spell did not work, she began to plead with him.

"Let me go, o good and kind man!" she said. "I will do anything you say."

"Will you go with me?"

"Anywhere you like."

Andrei turned homewards and took the Cat with him. When he came to his own tsardom he went to the palace with the Cat and said to the Tsar:

"I have done what you told me to do and brought Croon-Cat to you."

The Tsar could not believe his eyes.

"Come, Croon-Cat, show me fire and fury," he said.

At that the Cat began to sharpen her claws and glare at the Tsar, and made as if to rip open his breast and tear the living heart out of him. The Tsar was terrified.

"Do calm her, Andrei," he said.

Andrei quieted the Cat and locked her up in a cage, and then he went home to Tsarevna Maria. The two of them went on living happily together, but the Tsar grew more lovesick than ever. One day he sent for his Councillor again.

"You must think of some other way to get rid of Andrei the Archer. If you do not, I'll out with my sword and off with your head," said he.

The Councillor went straight to the tavern, sought out the ragamuffin, and asked him to help him out of his trouble. The ragamuffin tossed off his glass of wine, wiped his whiskers, and said:

"Go and tell the Tsar to make Andrei the Archer *go I know not where and fetch I know not what*. This task Andrei will never be able to fulfil, and so he will never come back."

The Councillor ran off to the Tsar and told him everything, word for word. The Tsar sent for Andrei.

"You have done me two services, now do me a third," he said *"Go I know not where and fetch I know not what*. If you do this, I shall reward you handsomely, if you do not, I'll out with my sword and off with your head."

Andrei went home, sat down on the bench and wept.

"Why are you so sad, dear heart?" asked Tsarevna Maria. "Has anything happened to grieve you so again?"

"Ah," said he, "your fair face will be my ruin. The Tsar has commanded me to *go I know not where and fetch I know not what*."

"Now that is a difficult task indeed. But never mind, go to bed; night is the mother of counsel."

Tsarevna Maria waited for midnight, and then she opened her book of spells. She read it through, flung it aside and clutched her head: the book did not tell her how to fulfil the Tsar's task. She went out on to the porch, took out a kerchief and waved it, and lo! all kinds of birds came flocking and all kinds of beasts came running to her.

"Hail, Beasts of the Forest and Birds of the Skies!" said she. "You beasts prowl everywhere, you birds fly everywhere—perhaps you can tell me how to *go I know not where and fetch I know not what*?"

But the birds and beasts replied:

"No, Tsarevna Maria, we cannot tell you that."

Tsarevna Maria waved her kerchief again, and the birds and beasts vanished as if they had never been. She waved it a third time, and two Giants appeared before her.

"What is your wish? What is your will?"

"My faithful servants, carry me to the middle of the Ocean-Sea."

The Giants lifted Tsarevna Maria, carried her to the Ocean-Sea and stood in the middle of the deep waters. There they stood like two tall columns, holding her up in their arms. Tsarevna Maria waved her kerchief and all the fishes and crawling things of the sea came swimming towards her.

"Fishes and Crawling Things of the Sea, you swim everywhere and know all the islands—perhaps you can tell me how to *go I know not where and fetch I know not what*?"

"No, Tsarevna Maria, we have never heard of such a place."

Tsarevna Maria grew sad and woebegone and she told the Giants to take her home. And the Giants carried her to Andrei's house and set her down on the door-step.

On the following morning Tsarevna Maria was up betimes to see Andrei off on his journey, and she gave him a ball of yarn and an embroidered towel.

"Throw the ball of yarn in front of you and follow it wherever it rolls," she said. "And wherever you are, take care, after you wash, not to wipe yourself with any towel but the one I have given you."

Andrei said good-bye to Tsarevna Maria, bowed to all sides of him and went out through the town gates. He threw the ball of yarn in front of him, and went after it as it rolled on and on.

The tale is short in telling, but the deed is long in doing. Many a tsardom and strange land did Andrei pass. The ball rolled on and, as the yarn unwound, it became smaller and smaller. Soon it was no bigger than a hen's egg; and after a time it became so small that you could hardly see it in the roadway.

Andrei came to a forest, he looked, and there before him was a little hut on hen's feet.

"Little hut, little hut, turn your back to the trees and your face to me, please," said Andrei.

The hut turned round, Andrei went in and saw an old hag sitting on a bench spinning tow.

"Ugh, ugh, Russian blood, never met by me before, now I smell it at my door. Who comes here? Where from? Where to? I will roast you alive, eat you up and roll over your bones."

"Come, come, old Baba-Yaga, fancy eating a wayfarer!" said Andrei. "A wayfarer is lean and tough and grey with dust. Heat the bath first, wash me and steam me, and then eat me up."

So Baba-Yaga heated the bath-house. Andrei washed and steamed himself and got out his wife's towel to dry himself.

"How did you come by that towel?" asked Baba-Yaga. "My daughter embroidered it."

"Your daughter is my wife. It was she who gave me the towel."

94

"Ah, welcome, dear son-in-law, welcome, and let me treat you to the best my house can offer!"

Baba-Yaga bestirred herself and set all kinds of foods, wines and other good things upon the table. Andrei sat down without any fuss and fell to, and Baba-Yaga sat down beside him and asked him how he had come to marry Tsarevna Maria and whether they were happy together. And Andrei told her all about everything, and about how the Tsar had sent him *he knew not where to fetch he knew not what.*

"If only you would help me, Mother!" he said.

"Ah, my dear son-in-law, even I have not heard of so strange a place. The only one who knows of such things is an Old Frog, and she has been living in the marsh these three hundred years. But never mind, go to bed; night is the mother of counsel."

Andrei went to bed, and Baba-Yaga took two birch brooms, flew to the marsh and called:

"Old Mother-Hopper, are you still alive?"

"I am."

"Then hop out of the marsh."

The Old Frog hopped out of the marsh and Baba-Yaga said:

"Do you know where *I know not what* is?"

"I do."

"Then be so kind as to tell me where it is. My son-in-law has been sent *I know not where to fetch I know not what.*"

"I would show him the way myself, but I am too old, it is a long hop," said the Frog. "Let your son-in-law put me into a jug of fresh milk and carry me to the Flaming River. There I shall tell him."

Baba-Yaga took Old Mother-Hopper, flew home, poured some fresh milk into a jug and put the Frog in it. Early next morning she woke Andrei up.

"Here is a jug with the Frog in it," she said. "Get dressed, mount my horse and go to the Flaming River. There you will leave the

96

horse and take the Frog out of the jug. She will tell you where to go."

Andrei dressed, took the jug and got on Baba-Yaga's horse. Whether they rode for a long or a little time nobody knows, but at last they came to the Flaming River. Across that river no beast could jump, no bird could fly. Andrei got off the horse, and the Frog said:

"Take me out of the jug, my fine handsome lad. We must cross the river."

Andrei took the Frog out of the jug and set her on the ground.

"Now climb on my back."

"Oh, but you are so tiny, Mother-Hopper, I will squash you."

"Have no fear of that. Get on and hold fast."

Andrei sat down on Old Mother-Hopper, and she began to puff herself up. She swelled and she swelled until she was as big as a haycock.

"Are you holding fast?" she asked.

"That I am, Mother."

Old Mother-Hopper swelled and swelled again until she was as big as a haystack.

"Are you holding fast?"

"Yes, Mother."

Again she swelled and swelled until she was taller than the dark forest. Then in one hop she was across the Flaming River. She set Andrei down on the other side and became her own little self again.

"Follow that path, my fine handsome lad, and you will see a tower that is not quite a tower, nor quite a hut, nor quite a barn, but a little bit of each. Go inside and stand behind the stove. There you will find *I know not what*."

Andrei went down the path and saw an old hut that was not quite a hut. It had no windows or porch, but was enclosed by a paling. In he went and hid behind the stove.

97

By and by there was a din and clatter in the woods, and in came, very quick and nimble, a little bearded man the size of a thimble, and bawled out:

"Hi, Brother Naoom, I'm hungry!"

Scarcely were the words out of his mouth when lo and behold! a table appeared as if out of thin air, and on the table stood a barrel of beer, very light and clear, and a roasted ox with a knife stuck into it. Quick-and-Nimble-the-Size-of-a-Thimble sat down before the ox, pulled out the sharp knife and began to cut the meat, sprinkle it with garlic and polish it off with gusto, praising the food as he ate.

He ate up every bit of the ox and drank the whole barrel of beer.

"Hi, Brother Naoom, clear the table!"

And all at once the table vanished as if it had never been there, bones, barrel and all. Andrei waited until Quick-and-Nimble-the-

Size-of-a-Thimble left, then he came out from behind the stove, plucked up courage and called:

"Brother Naoom, give me something to eat!"

Scarcely were the words out of his mouth when lo and behold! a table appeared as if out of thin air, and on it stood all kinds of foods and wines and other good things.

Andrei sat down at the table and said:

"Sit down, Brother Naoom, let us eat and drink together."

And an unseen voice answered:

"Thank you for your kindness, my friend. Many a year have I served here, yet never have I been given so much as a burnt crust, while you ask me to sit at your table."

Andrei watched and was stricken dumb with wonder. There was no one to be seen, yet the food vanished as if swept up with a broom; the wines and meads poured themselves into glasses and the glasses went clink-clank, hoppety-hop on the table.

"Brother Naoom, let me see you!" Andrei said.

"Nay, I am not to be seen. I am *I know not what.*"

"Brother Naoom, would you like to serve me?"

"Indeed I would. You are a good and a kind man if ever there was one."

When they had finished eating. Andrei said:

"Clear the table and come with me."

He went out of the hut and looked round.

"Are you here, Brother Naoom?"

"Yes. Do not be afraid, I shall never leave you."

By and by Andrei came to the Flaming River, where the Frog was waiting for him.

"Well, my fine handsome lad," said the Frog, "did you find *I know not what?*"

"Yes, Mother-Hopper."

"Get on my back."

Andrei got on her back again and the Frog began to puff herself up, till she was very, very big, and then she gave a hop and carried him across the Flaming River.

Andrei thanked Mother-Hopper and set off homewards. He would go on a bit, then turn round and ask:

"Are you here, Brother Naoom?"

"Yes. Do not be afraid, I shall never leave you."

Andrei walked and walked, and at last he grew weary and foot-sore.

"Oh, my," said he, "how tired I am!"

"Why did you not tell me before?" said Brother Naoom. "I could have got you home in no time."

And at once Andrei was caught up by a fierce gust of wind and whisked away over mountains and forests, over towns and villages. They flew over a deep sea, and Andrei was frightened.

"Brother Naoom, I should like to have a rest," said he.

The wind dropped at once and Andrei began to fall down into the sea. But where only blue waves had been splashing, he now saw an island, and on that island stood a palace with a golden roof and a beautiful garden all around it.

Said Brother Naoom to Andrei:

"Rest, eat, drink, and keep an eye on the sea. Three merchant ships will come sailing by. Hail them, invite the merchants to dinner and feast them royally—they have three marvels in their possession. Exchange me for those marvels—do not be afraid, I shall come back to you again."

Whether a long or a little time passed by nobody knows, but at last three ships came sailing from the West. The seafarers saw the island, and on it the palace with the golden roof and the beautiful garden all around it.

100

"What wonder is this?" said they. "Many a time have we sailed here, and never have we seen anything but the blue waves. Let us go ashore!"

The three ships cast anchor, and the three merchants got into a light boat and made for the island. And Andrei the Archer was on the shore, ready and waiting to greet them.

"Welcome, dear guests," said he.

The more the merchants saw, the greater was their wonder. The roof on the palace blazed like fire, birds sang in the trees and strange animals wandered about on the paths.

"Tell us, our good man, who built this wonder of wonders here?" the merchants asked.

"My servant, Brother Naoom, built it in a single night," Andrei replied.

He led the guests into the banquet hall, and said:

"Hi, Brother Naoom, give us something to eat and drink!"

All of a sudden—lo and behold!—a table appeared as if out of thin air, set with all the foods and wines the heart could desire. The merchants looked, and there was no end to their wonder and delight.

"Let us make an exchange, good man," said the merchants. "Give us your servant, Brother Naoom, and take any marvel you wish in return."

"Very well. What marvels can you offer?"

The first merchant took out a cudgel from under his coat. All one had to say was: "Now then, cudgel, give that man a trouncing!" and the cudgel would set to work and, no matter how strong he was, thrash the man to within an inch of his life.

The second merchant took out an axe from under his *caftan* and stood it on its handle, and the axe began to chop. Rap, tap—out came a ship; rap, tap—out came another, all complete with sails, and guns and sailors brave. The ships sailed, the guns fired and the brave sailors asked for orders.

He turned the axe upside down, and lo!—the ships vanished as if they had never been.

The third merchant took a reed pipe out of his pocket and blew upon it. And lo!—an army appeared, mounted and on foot, with rifles and cannon. The army marched, the bands played, the banners waved, and the horsemen galloped up and asked for orders.

Then the merchant blew into the other end of the pipe, and at once everything vanished.

"I like your marvels," said Andrei the Archer, "but mine is worth more. If you wish, I shall exchange Brother Naoom for all three of your marvels."

"Aren't you asking too much?"

"Please yourselves. It is that or nothing."

The merchants thought it over.

"What do we want with a cudgel, an axe and a pipe?" said they. "We had better exchange them for Brother Naoom; then we shall have all we want to eat and drink, night or day, without lifting a finger."

So the merchants gave Andrei the cudgel, the axe and the pipe, and shouted:

"Hi, Brother Naoom, you are coming with us! Will you serve us truly?"

"Why not?" came a voice. "It is all one to me whom I serve."

So the merchants went back to their ships and began to feast and make merry. They ate and drank, and they kept shouting:

"Step lively, Brother Naoom, bring us this, bring us that!"

They drank until they were dead drunk and dropped off to sleep where they sat.

And the Archer sat all by himself in the palace and felt very sad and miserable.

"Dear me," thought he, "I wonder where my faithful servant, Brother Naoom, is."

"Here I am. What do you wish?"

Andrei was overjoyed.

"Is it not time to go home, back to my young wife? Take me home, Brother Naoom."

And, as before, a blast of wind caught him up and carried him to his own land.

Now the merchants woke up, feeling sick and thirsty.

"Hi, Brother Naoom!" they shouted. "Give us something to eat and drink, and step lively!"

They called and shouted for a long time, but all in vain. They looked, and lo!—the island was gone. Only the blue waves splashed where it had stood.

The merchants were furious.

"What a bad man to have cheated us so!" they said.

But there was nothing they could do about it, so they weighed anchor and sailed off to wherever it was they were going.

Meanwhile Andrei the Archer flew home and alighted beside his hut. But where his hut had been there was now nothing but a charred chimney.

Andrei hung his head and went to a desolate spot by the blue sea. And there he was sitting and grieving when suddenly a blue-grey turtle-dove came flying up as if out of nowhere. It struck the ground and turned into his young wife, Tsarevna Maria.

They embraced and began asking each other questions and telling each other of all that had befallen them.

"Ever since you left home I have been flying about the woods and groves in the guise of a dove," said Tsarevna Maria. "Three times did the Tsar send for me, but they did not find me and so they burnt down our hut."

"Brother Naoom, can you raise a palace by the blue sea?" asked Andrei.

"Why not? It shall be done in the twinkling of an eye."

And true enough, before they could look round the palace was ready, and a grand palace it was, much better than the Tsar's. It stood in a great green garden and birds sang in the trees and all kinds of strange animals wandered about on the paths.

Andrei the Archer and Tsarevna Maria entered the palace, sat down by the window and began to talk, gazing at each other fondly the while. And so they lived without a care in the world for a day, and another, and a third.

Then the Tsar went out hunting and he saw a palace standing by the blue sea where nothing had stood before.

"What knave has built upon my land without my leave?" said he.

105

Off ran the Tsar's messengers, and when they came back they said that Andrei the Archer had built the palace and was living in it with his young wife, Tsarevna Maria.

The Tsar was angrier than ever, and he sent messengers to find out whether Andrei had been *I know not where and fetched I know not what.*

Off ran the messengers again, and when they came back they reported that Andrei the Archer had indeed been *I know not where and fetched I know not what.*

This sent the Tsar into a towering rage. He had his troops mustered and sent down to the sea, and commanded that the palace be razed to the ground and Andrei the Archer and Tsarevna Maria put to a cruel death.

Andrei saw what a powerful army was coming against him, so he whisked out his axe and stood it on its handle. Rap, tap, went the axe,

and a ship stood upon the sea; rap, tap, and there was another ship. The axe went rap-tap a hundred times till a hundred ships sailed upon the blue sea.

Andrei got out his pipe and blew on it—and an army appeared, mounted and on foot, with rifles, cannon and flying banners.

The captains galloped up and awaited orders, and Andrei ordered them to begin battle. The bands started playing, the drums rolled and the regiments moved into attack. The foot soldiers broke the ranks of the Tsar's army, and the horsemen galloped about taking prisoners. And the fleet of a hundred ships turned its cannon on the Tsar's town.

When the Tsar saw his troops fleeing, he rushed to stop them. At this Andrei got out his cudgel.

"Now then, cudgel, break the Tsar's bones for him!"

And off the cudgel went with a hop and a skip across the field. It caught up with the Tsar and struck him on the forehead and he fell down dead.

And that was the end of the battle. The people flocked out of the town and begged Andrei the Archer to take the rule of the realm in his hands.

To this Andrei agreed. He gave a grand feast, the like of which the world had never seen, and together with Tsarevna Maria he ruled the realm to the end of his days.

Little Girl and the Swan-Geese

Once there was a peasant and his wife and they had a little girl and a little boy.

"Daughter," said the Mother to her Little Girl, "we are going out to work, so look after your Little Brother. If you are a good girl and do not run out into the street we shall buy you a new kerchief."

Father and Mother went away, and Little Girl never stopped to think about what she had been told. She seated Little Brother on the grass under the window, ran out into the street and began to play with her friends, forgetting all about everything.

Suddenly a flock of Swan-Geese came flying up. They swooped down, caught up Little Brother and carried him off on their wings.

Little Girl came home, she looked, but alas!—Little Brother was gone. She ran here and there, but not a sign of him did she find.

She began calling him, and she wept and sobbed, crying that she would catch it from Father and Mother, but Little Brother did not reply.

She ran out into the open field but there was nothing she could see save some Swan-Geese flying beyond the dark forest. She knew then that it was they who had carried off her brother: folks said the Swan-Geese were wicked birds who stole little children.

So away ran Little Girl after the birds. She ran and she ran till she came to an Oven.

"Oven, Oven, tell me where the Swan-Geese have flown."

"Eat one of my rye cakes and I will tell you," said the Oven.

"What, me eat a rye cake? At home we do not eat even wheaten cakes!"

So the Oven did not tell her. Little Girl ran on a bit farther and saw an Apple-Tree.

"Apple-Tree, Apple-Tree, tell me where the Swan-Geese have flown."

"Eat one of my wild apples and I will tell you," said the Tree.

"At home we do not eat even garden apples!"

So the Apple-Tree did not tell her. Little Girl ran on till she came to Milk River with Jelly Banks.

"Milk River with Jelly Banks, tell me where the Swan-Geese have flown."

"Have some of my jelly with milk and I will tell you."

"At home we do not eat even jelly with cream."

So Milk River did not tell her.

Little Girl ran about the fields and woods for a long, long time. And now day was giving way to evening, and there was nothing for her to do but go home. All at once, what should she

see but a hut on hen's feet, very tidy and neat, turning round and round without a sound.

The hut had one window, and inside the hut sat Baba-Yaga, the witch, spinning tow. And on the bench sat Little Brother playing with silver apples.

Little Girl went in.

"Good evening, Granny!"

"Good evening, lass. What brings you here?"

"In the fields and woods have I walked all day, over marshes and swamps have I made my way. My frock is wet through, so I've come to you to get warm."

"Sit down then and spin some tow."

Baba-Yaga gave Little Girl the spindle and herself went out. And Little Girl sat there spinning when all of a sudden a Mouse ran out from under the stove and said to her:

"Lassie, lassie, give me some porridge and I will tell you something."

Little Girl gave it some porridge, and Mouse said:

"Baba-Yaga has gone to light a fire in the bath-house. She will steam you and wash you, roast you in the oven and eat you up, and then roll around on your bones."

Little Girl sat there more dead than alive, and she wept and sobbed, but Mouse went on:

"Make haste, take Little Brother and run away, and I will spin the tow for you."

So Little Girl took Little Brother in her arms and ran off. Baba-Yaga came up to the window every once in a while and asked:

"Are you spinning, lass?"

And Mouse would answer: "Yes, I am, Granny."

Baba-Yaga made a fire in the bath-house and came for Little Girl. But the hut was empty.

Baba-Yaga cried: "Off you go, Swan-Geese, fly and catch them! Little Girl has carried off Little Brother!"

Little Girl ran until she came to Milk River, and what should she see but the Swan-Geese coming after her and Little Brother.

"Milk River, Milk River, hide me, do!" cried Little Girl.

"Eat some of my plain fruit jelly."

Little Girl ate some and said thank you. So Milk River hid her and her brother in the shadow of its Fruit-Jelly Banks.

And the Swan-Geese never saw them and flew past.

Little Girl ran on again. But the Swan-Geese turned back and flew straight towards her. At any moment they might see her.

What was Little Girl to do? On she ran and she came across the Apple-Tree.

"Apple-Tree, Apple-Tree, hide me, do!"

"Eat my wild apples."

Little Girl ate one quickly and said thank you, and the Apple-Tree hid her and Little Brother among its leaves and branches.

The Swan-Geese never saw them and flew past.

Little Girl picked up her brother and ran on again. She ran and she ran and she had almost reached home when the Swan-Geese caught sight of her. They honked and flapped their wings,

and in another minute would have torn Little Brother out of her arms.

Little Girl ran up to the Oven.

"Oven, Oven, hide me, do!"

"Eat one of my rye cakes."

Little Girl popped a piece of cake into her mouth and herself crawled into the Oven with her brother.

The Swan-Geese flew round and round screaming and honking, but after a while they gave it up and flew back to Baba-Yaga.

Little Girl said thank you to the Oven and ran home with her brother.

And before long Father and Mother came home too.

The Silver Saucer
and the Rosy-Cheeked Apple

O nce upon a time there lived an old man and an old woman and they had three daughters. The two elder daughters liked to dress up in fancy clothes and to play games and make merry, but the younger daughter was quiet and modest in all her ways. The elder daughters wore bright, flowered *sarafans*, and gilded beads, and boots with high, carved heels. But Masha's gowns were as dark as her eyes were light and clear. Her one beauty was her hair which fell to the ground in a golden plait and brushed the flowers that grew in her path as she walked. The elder daughters were lazy and sat about doing nothing like two grand ladies, but Masha was busy around the house and in the field and garden from morning till night. She would weed the vegetables and chop firewood for splinters to light the house with and milk the cows and feed the ducks. A person had only to ask and Masha would come running to bring whatever it was he wanted. Never would she cross anyone by so much as a word and she was always ready to do everyone's bidding. Her sisters would order her about and make her do their chores for them, and she would do them and say nothing.

And so it went.

One day, the old man made ready to take some hay to market, and he promised to bring back gifts for his daughters.

Said the first daughter:

"Buy me a length of blue silk for a *sarafan*, Father."

Said the second daughter:

"Buy me a length of red velvet."

But Masha said nothing.

The old man took pity on her.

"What shall I buy for you, Masha, my child?" he asked her.

"Well, Father dear, I should like a rosy-cheeked apple and a silver saucer."

At this Masha's sisters burst out laughing, and they laughed so hard that they all but split their sides.

"What a little fool you are, Masha!" they cried. "Why, we have a whole orchard of apples, you can pick any you please. And as for the saucer, what do you need it for—to feed the ducklings?"

"No, sisters dear. I shall roll the apple over the saucer and say magic words over it. An old beggar woman taught me them for giving her a *kalach*."

At that they laughed harder than ever, and the old man said to them:

"Now that's enough. I won't have you laughing at your sister. And I shall bring all of you gifts after your own hearts."

Whether he went far or near and whether he was long away or not no one knows, but the old man sold his hay and he bought his three daughters their gifts. To the first daughter he brought a length of blue silk, to the second daughter, a length of red velvet, and to Masha, a silver saucer and a rosy-cheeked apple.

The two elder sisters were overjoyed. They set to making their *sarafans* and they laughed at Masha.

"Sit there with your apple, you little fool," said they to her.

And Masha sat down in a corner of the hut, she rolled her rosy-cheeked apple over her silver saucer, and she began to sing and chant:

"Roll, roll, rosy apple, over the silver saucer, show me towns and leas, show me forests and seas, show me mountains high and the blue-blue sky, show me all of Rus, of my own dear land!"

116

All of a sudden there came a ringing as of bells and the whole hut was flooded with light. Over the silver saucer rolled the rosy-cheeked apple and on the saucer, as clear as in real life, there appeared towns and vales, hills and dales, soldiers in the fields with swords and shields, grassy leas, ships on the seas, mountains high and the blue-blue sky. In the sky the bright sun sailed after the pale moon, and the stars danced in a ring, and on the lakes the swans sang their songs.

The sisters looked and turned green with envy. Their only thought now was to find a way of wheedling the saucer and apple out of Masha.

But Masha wanted nothing, would take nothing, and went on playing with her apple and saucer every evening.

One day, the sisters decided to lure her into the forest, and they said to Masha:

"Come, dear heart, come, sweet sister, let us go gathering berries in the forest. We'll bring back some wild strawberries for Mother and Father."

They went to the forest, but there were no berries to be seen anywhere. Masha took out her silver saucer, rolled her rosy-cheeked apple over it and said in a singsong voice:

"Roll, rosy apple, over the silver saucer, roll and show me where the wild strawberries are growing and the sky-blue flowers are blooming."

All at once there came a pealing of bells, the rosy-cheeked apple rolled over the silver saucer and on the saucer, as clear as in real life, the forest and all its secret nooks appeared: the glades where the wild strawberries grew, the sky-blue flowers bloomed, the mushrooms hid and the springs gushed, and the lakes where the swans sang.

And Masha's two mean-hearted sisters watched and were filled with such envy that their sight grew dim. They caught up a knobby stick and they killed Masha with it. They buried her underneath a birch-tree and took the silver saucer and rosy-cheeked apple for themselves. It was evening by the time they reached home, bringing baskets full of mushrooms and berries, and they said to their mother and father:

"Masha ran away from us and got lost. We looked all over the forest, but could not find her. The wolves must have eaten her up in the thicket."

The mother burst into tears, and the father said:

"Roll the apple over the saucer and, perhaps, it will show us where our Masha is."

The sisters turned cold with fear, but they had to do as their father bade. They rolled the apple over the saucer, but the apple would not roll and the saucer would not spin and there was nothing to be seen on it: neither forests nor fields, neither mountains high nor the blue-blue sky.

Now at that very time and hour a young shepherd was out in the forest looking for a sheep that had strayed away from the flock, and he came upon a white birch-tree with a freshly-heaped mound of turf beneath it and sky-blue flowers growing all around. Shooting up amongst the flowers were some long, slender reeds. The shepherd cut himself a reed and made a pipe out of it. But no sooner had he brought the pipe to his lips than it began to play of itself and to sing out:

"Play, pipe, play for the shepherd to hear, sweet songs and gay, the shepherd to cheer! As for me, poor lass, they killed me, alas, for a silver saucer, for a rosy-cheeked apple."

The shepherd was frightened, and he ran straight to the village and told the villagers all about it. And they gathered round to hear him and gasped in horror.

Masha's father, too, came running up. And the moment he picked up the pipe it started playing of itself and singing:

"Play, pipe, play for my father to hear, sweet songs and gay, my father to cheer! As

for me, poor lass, they killed me, alas, for a silver saucer, for a rosy-cheeked apple."

The father began to weep.

"Take us to where you cut the reed for your pipe, shepherd," he said.

The shepherd led them to the mound in the forest, and there were sky-blue flowers growing beneath the birch-tree and tomtits perching on its boughs and singing away. They dug up the mound, and there beneath it lay Masha, dead, but looking more beautiful than ever. She seemed to be asleep, poor maid, for on her cheeks the roses played. And the pipe went on playing and singing:

"Play, pipe, play, sad songs and gay. Listen, Father, to what I say. By my sisters was I to the forest ta'en, by my sisters was I in the forest slain. Play, pipe, play, sad songs and gay. Listen, Father, to what I say. If you wish to see me alive and well, fetch some crystal water from the Tsar's own well."

At this, Masha's two black-hearted sisters trembled and turned pale, they fell on their knees and confessed their crime. And they were put away behind locks of iron to await the Tsar's orders, his high decree.

The old man made ready and set off for the Tsar's city to fetch the living water.

Whether a long time passed by or a little time nobody knows, but he finally reached the Tsar's city and came to the Tsar's palace just as the Tsar was coming down from his porch of gold.

The old man bowed to the ground and told the Tsar all about everything.

Said the Tsar:

"You may take some living water from my well, old man, and when your daughter comes to life, bring her to me together with the two vipers, her sisters, and mind she does not forget to take along her silver saucer and rosy-cheeked apple."

The old man was overjoyed and bowed to the ground again many times, and he took home with him a phial of the living water.

No sooner had he sprayed Masha with the living water than she came alive again and clung to him as tenderly as a dove.

The people came running up and they rejoiced in the sight.

And now the old man set off again for the Tsar's city with his three daughters. He arrived there in due time and was led into the palace.

The Tsar came in and he glanced at Masha. There she stood as lovely as a spring flower, her eyes as bright as the rays of the sun, her face as fair as the sky at dawn, and the tears rolling down her cheeks like the purest of pearls.

"Where is your silver saucer and rosy-cheeked apple?" asked the Tsar of Masha.

And Masha took them out, and she rolled the rosy-cheeked apple over the silver saucer.

All of a sudden there came a great ringing of bells, and one after another Russian cities and towns appeared on the saucer. Into the

towns the regiments streamed with their battle flags flowing, and formed into fighting order, the captains standing in front of the lines, the *sotniks*, in front of the hundreds, and the *desyatniks*, in front of columns of ten. And such was the firing and shooting, so thick the smoke, that the field of battle was hid from sight as if the day had turned into night.

The rosy-cheeked apple rolled over the silver saucer, and on the saucer the sea appeared, rising in waves, with the ships sailing on it as smoothly as swans, the flags waving and the cannon barking. And such was the firing and shooting, so thick the smoke, that all was soon hid from sight as if the day had turned into night.

The rosy-cheeked apple rolled over the silver saucer, and on the saucer the sky appeared in all its beauty: the bright sun sailed after the pale crescent moon, the stars danced in a ring and the swans up in the clouds sang their songs.

The Tsar was filled with wonder at so rare a sight, but Masha wept and wept and could not stop.

Said she to the Tsar:

"Take my rosy-cheeked apple and my silver saucer, only pardon my sisters, do not put them to death because of me."

And the Tsar lifted her up from her knees and said:

"Your saucer is of silver, but your heart is of gold. Will you be my own dear wife and a kind and gentle Tsaritsa for my tsardom? And as for your sisters, I shall pardon them since you ask me to."

There was no need to brew beer or to make wine, for the Tsar's cellars overflowed with both, and so the wedding was held without further ado, and a feast to celebrate it. To say the least, 'twas a right noble feast. So loud did they play without pause or stop that the stars from the sky began to drop. So hard did they dance, as I hear tell, that they broke their heels and the floor as well.

And that, dear friend, is the tale's end.

Emelya and the Pike

nce upon a time there lived an old man who had three sons, two of them clever young men and the third, Emelya, a fool.

The two elder brothers were always at work, while Emelya lay on the stove ledge all day long with not a care in the world.

One day the two brothers rode away to market, and their wives said:

"Go and fetch some water, Emelya."

And Emelya, lying on the stove ledge, replied:

"Not I. I don't want to."

"Go, Emelya, or your brothers will bring no presents for you from the market."

"Oh, all right then."

Down climbed Emelya from the stove, put on his boots and *caftan* and, taking along two pails and an axe, went to the river.

He cut a hole in the ice with his axe, scooped up two pailfuls of water, put down the pails and himself bent down to look into the ice-hole. He looked and he looked and what did he see but a Pike swimming in the water. Out shot his arm, and there was the Pike in his hands.

"We'll have some fine pike soup for dinner to-day!" he exclaimed, delighted.

But the Pike suddenly spoke up in a human voice and said:

"Let me go, Emelya, and I'll do you a good turn, too, some day"

Emelya only laughed.

"What good turn could you do me? No, I think I'll take you home and tell my sisters-in-law to make some soup. I do so love pike soup."

But the Pike fell to begging him again and said:

"Do let me go, Emelya, and I'll do anything you wish."

"All right," Emelya replied, "only first you must prove you aren't trying to fool me."

Said the Pike: "Tell me what you want, Emelya."

"I want my pails to go home all by themselves without spilling a drop of water."

"Very well, Emelya," the Pike said. "Whenever you wish something, you have only to say:

"By will of the Pike, do as I like', and it will all be done at once."

And Emelya, nothing loath, said:

"By will of the Pike, do as I like! Off you go home, pails, by yourselves!"

And, lo and behold! the pails turned and marched up the hill.

Emelya put the Pike back into the ice-hole and himself walked after his pails.

On went the pails along the village street, and the villagers stood round and marvelled while Emelya followed the pails, chuckling. The pails marched straight into Emelya's hut and jumped up on the bench, and Emelya climbed up on to the stove ledge again.

A long time passed by and a little time, and his sisters-in-law said to Emelya:

"Why are you lying there, Emelya? Go and chop us some wood."

"Not I. I don't want to," Emelya said.

"If you don't do what we say, your brothers will bring no presents for you from the market."

Emelya was loath to leave the stove ledge. He remembered the Pike and said under his breath:

"By will of the Pike, do as I like! Go and chop some wood, axe, and you, wood, come inside the house and jump into the stove."

And lo! the axe leapt out from under the bench and into the yard and began to chop the wood, and the logs filed into the hut all by themselves and jumped into the stove.

A long time passed by and a little time, and his sisters-in-law said to Emelya:

"We have no more wood, Emelya. Go to the forest and cut some."

And Emelya, lolling on the stove, replied:

"And what are you here for?"

"What do you mean by that, Emelya?" the women said. "Surely it's not our business to go to the forest for wood."

"But I don't much want to do it," Emelya said.

"Well, then you won't get any presents," they told him.

There was no help for it, so Emelya climbed down from the stove and put on his boots and *caftan*. He took a length of rope and an axe, came out into the yard and, getting into the sledge, cried:

"Open the gates, women!"

And his sisters-in-law said to him:

"What are you doing in the sledge, fool? You haven't harnessed the horse yet."

"I can do without the horse," Emelya replied.

His sisters-in-law opened the gate and Emelya said under his breath:

"By will of the Pike, do as I like! Off you go to the forest, sledge!"

And, lo and behold! the sledge whizzed out through the gate so quickly that one could scarcely have caught up with it even on horseback.

Now the way to the forest lay through a town, and the sledge knocked down many people. The townsfolk cried: "Hold him! Catch him!" But Emelya paid no heed and only urged the sledge on to go the faster.

He came to the forest, stopped the sledge and said:

"By will of the Pike, do as I like! Cut some dry wood, axe, and you, faggots, climb into the sledge and bind yourselves together."

And, lo and behold! the axe began to hack and split the dry wood,

126

and the faggots dropped into the sledge one by one and bound themselves together. Emelya then ordered the axe to cut him a cudgel, so heavy that one could scarcely lift it. He got up on top of his load and said:

"By will of the Pike, do as I like! Off you go home, sledge!"

And the sledge drove off very fast indeed. Emelya again passed through the town where he had knocked down so many people, and there they were all ready and waiting for him. They seized him, pulled him out of the sledge and began to curse and to beat him.

Seeing that he was in a bad plight, Emelya said under his breath:

"By will of the Pike, do as I like! Come, cudgel, give them a good thrashing!"

And the cudgel sprang up and laid to, right and left. The townsfolk took to their heels and Emelya went home and climbed up on the stove again.

A long time passed by and a little time, and the Tsar heard of Emelya's doings and sent one of his officers to find him and bring him to the palace.

The officer came to Emelya's village, entered his hut and asked him:

"Are you Emelya the Fool?"

And Emelya replied from the stove ledge:

"What if I am?"

"Dress quickly and I shall take you to the Tsar's palace."

"Oh, no. I don't want to go," Emelya said.

The officer flew into a temper and struck Emelya in the face. And Emelya said under his breath:

"By will of the Pike, do as I like! Come, cudgel, give him a good thrashing."

And out the cudgel jumped and beat the officer so that it was all he could do to drag himself back to the palace.

The Tsar was much surprised to learn that his officer had not been able to get the better of Emelya and he sent for the greatest of his nobles.

"Find Emelya and bring him to my palace or I'll have your head chopped off," he said.

The great noble bought a store of raisins and prunes and honey cakes, and then he came to the selfsame village and into the selfsame hut and he asked Emelya's sisters-in-law what it was Emelya liked best.

"Emelya likes to be spoken to kindly," they said. "He will do anything you want if only you are gentle with him and promise him a red *caftan* for a present."

The great noble then gave Emelya the raisins, prunes and honey cakes he had brought, and said:

"Please, Emelya, why do you lie on the stove ledge? Come with me to the Tsar's palace."

"I'm well enough where I am," Emelya replied.

"Ah, Emelya, the Tsar will feast you on sweetmeats and wines. Do let us go to the palace."

"Not I. I don't want to," Emelya replied.

"But, Emelya, the Tsar will give you a fine red *caftan* for a present and a cap and a pair of boots."

Emelya thought for a while and then he said:

"Very well, then, I shall come. Only you must go on alone and I shall follow by and by."

The noble rode away and Emelya lay on the stove a while longer and then said:

"By will of the Pike, do as I like! Off you go to the Tsar's palace, stove!"

And lo! the corners of the hut began to crack, the roof swayed, a wall crashed down and the stove whipped off all by itself into the street and down the road and made straight for the Tsar's palace.

The Tsar looked out of the window and marvelled.

"What is that?" he asked.

And the great noble replied:

"That is Emelya riding on his stove to your palace."

The Tsar stepped out on his porch and said:

"I have had many complaints about you, Emelya. It seems you have knocked down many people."

"Why did they get in the way of my sledge?" said Emelya.

Now, the Tsar's daughter Tsarevna Marya was looking out of the palace window just then, and when Emelya saw her, he said under his breath:

"By will of the Pike, do as I like! Let the Tsar's daughter fall in love with me."

And he added:

"Go home, stove!"

The stove turned and made straight for Emelya's village. It whisked into the hut and went back to its place, and Emelya lay on the stove ledge as before.

Meanwhile, there were tears and wails in the palace. Tsarevna Marya was crying her eyes out for Emelya. She told her father she could not live without him and begged him to let her marry Emelya. The Tsar was much troubled and grieved and he said to the great noble:

"Go and bring Emelya here, dead or alive. Do not fail, or I'll have your head chopped off."

The great noble bought many kinds of dainties and sweet wines and set off for Emelya's village again. He entered the selfsame hut and he began to feast Emelya royally.

Emelya had his fill of the good food and the wine, and his head swimming, lay down and fell asleep. And the noble put the sleeping Emelya into his carriage and rode off with him to the Tsar's palace.

The Tsar at once ordered a large barrel bound with iron hoops to be brought in. Emelya and Tsarevna Marya were placed into it and the barrel was tarred and cast into the sea.

A long time passed by and a little time, and Emelya awoke. Finding himself in darkness and closely confined, he said:

"Where am I?"

130

And Tsarevna Marya replied:

"Sad and dreary is our lot, Emelya my love! They have put us in a tarred barrel and cast us into the blue sea."

"And who are you?" Emelya asked.

"I am Tsarevna Marya."

Said Emelya:

"By will of the Pike, do as I like! Come, o wild winds, cast the barrel on to the dry shore and let it rest on the yellow sand!"

And, lo and behold! the wild winds began to blow, the sea became troubled and the barrel was cast on to the dry shore and it came to rest on the yellow sand. Out stepped Emelya and Tsarevna Marya, and Tsarevna Marya said:

"Where are we going to live, Emelya my love? Do build us a hut of some kind."

"Not I. I don't want to," Emelya replied.

But she begged and begged and at last he said:

"By will of the Pike, do as I like! Let a palace of stone with a roof of gold be built!"

And no sooner were the words out of his mouth than a stone palace with a roof of gold rose up before them. Round it there spread a green garden, where flowers bloomed and birds sang. Tsarevna Marya and Emelya came into the palace and sat down by the window.

Said Tsarevna Marya:

"Oh, Emelya, couldn't you become a little more handsome?"

And Emelya did not think long before he said:

"By will of the Pike, do as I like! Change me into a tall and handsome man."

And lo! Emelya turned into a youth as fair as the sky at dawn, the handsomest youth that ever was born.

Now about that time the Tsar went hunting and he saw a palace where one had never been seen before.

"What dolt has dared to build a palace on my ground?" he asked, and he sent his messengers to learn who the culprit was.

The Tsar's messengers ran to the palace, stood under the window and called to Emelya, asking him to tell them who he was.

"Tell the Tsar to come and visit me, and he shall hear from my lips who I am," Emelya replied.

The Tsar did as Emelya bade, and Emelya met him at the palace gate, led him into the palace, seated him at his table and feasted him royally. The Tsar ate and drank and marvelled.

"Who are you, my good fellow?" he asked at last.

"Do you remember Emelya the Fool who came to visit you on top of a stove?" Emelya said. "Do you remember how you had him put in a tarred barrel together with your daughter Tsarevna Marya and cast into the sea? Well, I am that same Emelya. If I choose, I can set fire to your whole tsardom and level it with the ground."

The Tsar was very frightened and he begged Emelya to forgive him.

"You can have my daughter in marriage and you can have my tsardom, too, only spare me, Emelya," said he.

Then such a grand feast was held as the world had never seen. Emelya married Tsarevna Marya and began to rule the realm and they both lived happily ever after.

And that is my faithful tale's end, while he who listened is my own true friend.

The Frog Tsarevna

L ong, long ago there was a Tsar who had three
sons. One day, when his sons were grown to
manhood, the Tsar called them to him and said:

"My dear sons, while yet I am not old I should
like to see you married and to rejoice in the sight of your children and
my grandchildren."

And the sons replied:

"If that is your wish, Father, then give us your blessing. Who
would you like us to marry?"

"Now then, my sons, you must each of you take an arrow and go
out into the open field. You must shoot the arrows, and wherever
they fall, there will you find your destined brides."

The sons bowed to their father and, each of them taking an arrow,
went out into the open field. There they drew their bows and let
fly their arrows.

The eldest son's arrow fell in a boyar's courtyard and was picked
up by the boyar's daughter. The middle son's arrow fell in a rich
merchant's yard and was picked up by the merchant's daughter. And
as for the youngest son, Tsarevich Ivan, his arrow shot up and flew
away he knew not where. He went in search of it and he walked
on and on till he reached a marsh, and what did he see sitting there

135

but a Frog with the arrow in its mouth. Said Tsarevich Ivan to the Frog:

"Frog, Frog, give me back my arrow."

But the Frog replied:

"I will if you marry me!"

"What do you mean, how can I marry a frog!"

"You must, for I am your destined bride."

Tsarevich Ivan felt sad and crestfallen. But there was nothing to be done, and he picked up the Frog and carried it home.

Three weddings were celebrated: his eldest son the Tsar married to the boyar's daughter, his middle son, to the merchant's daughter, and poor Tsarevich Ivan, to the Frog.

Some little time passed, and the Tsar called his sons to his side.

"I want to see which of your wives is the better needle-woman," said he. "Let them each make me a shirt by tomorrow morning."

The sons bowed to their father and left him.

Tsarevich Ivan came home, sat down and hung his head. And the Frog hopped over the floor and up to him and asked:

"Why do you hang your head, Tsarevich Ivan? What is it that troubles you?"

"Father bids you make him a shirt by tomorrow morning."

Said the Frog:

"Do not grieve, Tsarevich Ivan, but go to bed, for morning is wiser than evening."

Tsarevich Ivan went to bed, and the Frog hopped out on to the porch, cast off its frog skin and turned into Vasilisa the Wise and Clever, a maiden fair beyond compare.

She clapped her hands and cried:

"Come, my women and maids, make haste and set to work! Make me a shirt by tomorrow morning, like those my own father used to wear."

136

In the morning Tsarevich Ivan awoke, and there was the Frog hopping on the floor again, but the shirt was all ready and lying on the table wrapped in a handsome towel. Tsarevich Ivan was overjoyed. He took the shirt and he went with it to his father who was busy receiving his two elder sons' gifts. The eldest son laid out his shirt, and the Tsar took it and said:

"This shirt will only do for a poor peasant to wear.'

The middle son laid out his shirt, and the Tsar said:

"This shirt will only do to go to the baths in."

Then Tsarevich Ivan laid out his shirt, all beautifully embroidered in gold and silver, and the Tsar took one look at it and said:

"Now that is a shirt to wear on holidays!"

The two elder brothers went home and they spoke among themselves and said:

"It seems we were wrong to laugh at Tsarevich Ivan's wife. She is no frog, but a witch."

Now the Tsar again called his sons.

"Let your wives bake me some bread by tomorrow morning," said he. "I want to know which of them is the best cook."

Tsarevich Ivan hung his head and went home And the Frog asked him:

"Why are you so sad, Tsarevich Ivan?"

Said Tsarevich Ivan:

"You are to bake some bread for my father by tomorrow morning."

"Do not grieve, Tsarevich Ivan, but go to bed. Morning is wiser than evening."

And her two sisters-in-law, who had laughed at the Frog at first, now sent an old woman who worked in the kitchen to see how she baked her bread.

But the Frog was clever and guessed what they were up to. She kneaded some dough, broke off the top of the stove and threw the dough down the hole. The old woman ran to the two sisters-in-law and told them all about it, and they did as the Frog had done.

And the Frog hopped out on to the porch, turned into Vasilisa the Wise and Clever and clapped her hands.

"Come, my women and maids, make haste and set to work!" cried she. "By tomorrow morning bake me some soft white bread, the kind I used to eat at my own father's house."

138

In the morning Tsarevich Ivan woke up, and there was the bread all ready, lying on the table and prettily decorated with all manner of things: stamped figures on the sides and towns with walls and gates on the top.

Tsarevich Ivan was overjoyed. He wrapped up the bread in a towel and took it to his father who was just receiving the loaves his elder sons had brought. Their wives had dropped the dough into the stove as the old woman had told them to do, and the loaves came out charred and lumpy.

The Tsar took the bread from his eldest son, he looked at it and he sent it to the servants' hall. He took the bread from his middle son, and he did the same with it. But when Tsarevich Ivan handed him his bread, the Tsar said:

"Now that is bread to be eaten only on holidays!"

And the Tsar bade his three sons come and feast with him on the morrow together with their wives.

Once again Tsarevich Ivan came home sad and sorrowful, and he hung his head very low. And the Frog hopped over the floor and up to him and said:

"Croak, croak, why are you so sad, Tsarevich Ivan? Is it that your father has grieved you by an unkind word?"

"Oh, Frog, Frog!" cried Tsarevich Ivan. "How can I help being sad? The Tsar has ordered me to bring you to his feast, and how can I show you to people!"

Said the Frog in reply:

"Do not grieve, Tsarevich Ivan, but go to the feast alone, and I will follow later. When you hear a great tramping and thundering, do not be afraid, but if they ask you what it is, say: 'That is my Frog riding in her box.'"

So Tsarevich Ivan went to the feast alone, and his elder brothers came with the wives who were all dressed up in their finest clothes and had their brows blackened and roses painted on their cheeks. They stood there, and they made fun of Tsarevich Ivan.

"Why have you come without your wife?" asked they. "You could have brought her in a handkerchief. Wherever did you find such a beauty? You must have searched all the swamps for her."

Now the Tsar with his sons and his daughters-in-law and all the guests sat down to feast at the oaken tables covered with embroidered cloths. Suddenly there came a great tramping and thundering, and the whole palace shook and trembled. The guests were frightened and jumped up from their seats. But Tsarevich Ivan said:

"Do not fear, honest folk. That is only my Frog riding in her box."

140

And there dashed up to the porch to the Tsar's palace a gilded carriage drawn by six white horses, and out of it stepped Vasilisa the Wise and Clever. Her gown of sky-blue silk was studded with stars, and on her head she wore the bright crescent moon, and so beautiful was she that it could not be pictured and could not be told, but was a true wonder and joy to behold! She took Tsarevich Ivan by the hand and led him to the oaken tables covered with embroidered cloths.

The guests began eating and drinking and making merry. Vasilisa the Wise and Clever drank from her glass and poured the dregs into her left sleeve. She ate some swan meat and threw the bones into her right sleeve.

And the wives of the elder sons saw what she did and they did the same.

They ate and drank and then the time came to dance. Vasilisa the Wise and Clever took Tsarevich Ivan by the hand and began to dance. She danced and she whirled and she circled round and round, and everyone watched and marvelled. She waved her left sleeve, and a lake appeared; she waved her right sleeve, and white swans began to swim upon the lake. The Tsar and his guests were filled with wonder.

Then the wives of the two elder sons began dancing. They waved their left sleeves, and only splashed mead over the guests; they waved their right sleeves, and bones flew about on all sides, and one bone hit the Tsar in the eye. And the Tsar was very angry and told both his daughters-in-law to get out of his sight.

In the meantime, Tsarevich Ivan slipped out, ran home and, finding the frog skin, threw it in the stove and burnt it.

Now Vasilisa the Wise and Clever came home, and she at once saw that her frog skin was gone. She sat down on a bench, very sad and sorrowful, and she said to Tsarevich Ivan:

"Ah, Tsarevich Ivan, what have you done! Had you but waited just three more days, I would have been yours for ever. But now farewell. Seek me beyond the Thrice-Nine Lands in the Thrice-Ten Tsardom where lives Koshchei the Deathless."

And Vasilisa the Wise and Clever turned into a grey cuckoo-bird and flew out of the window. Tsarevich Ivan cried and wept for a long time and then he bowed to all sides of him and went off he knew not where to seek his wife, Vasilisa the Wise and Clever. Whether he walked far or near, for a long time or a little time, no one knows, but his boots were worn, his *caftan* frayed and torn, and his cap battered by the rain. After a while he met a little old man who was as old as old can be.

"Good morrow, good youth!" quoth he. "What do you seek and whither are you bound?"

Tsarevich Ivan told him of his trouble, and the little old man, who was as old as old can be, said:

"Ah, Tsarevich Ivan, why did you burn the frog skin? It was not yours to wear or to do away with. Vasilisa the Wise and Clever was born wiser and cleverer than her father, and this so angered him that he turned her into a frog for three years. Ah, well, it can't be helped now. Here is a ball of thread for you. Follow it without fear wherever it rolls."

Tsarevich Ivan thanked the little old man who was as old as old can be, he went after the ball of thread, and he followed it wherever it rolled. In an open field he met a bear. He took aim and was about to kill it, but the bear spoke up in a human voice and said:

"Do not kill me, Tsarevich Ivan, who knows but you may have need of me some day."

Tsarevich Ivan took pity on the bear, let him go and himself went on. By and by he looked, and lo!—there was a drake flying overhead. Tsarevich Ivan took aim, but the drake said to him in a human voice:

"Do not kill me, Tsarevich Ivan, who knows but you may have need of me some aay!"

And Tsarevich Ivan spared the drake and went on. Just then a hare came running. Tsarevich Ivan took aim quickly and was about to shoot it, but the hare said in a human voice:

"Do not kill me, Tsarevich Ivan, who knows but you may have need of me some day!"

And Tsarevich Ivan spared the hare and went farther. He came to the blue sea and he saw a pike lying on the sandy shore and gasping for breath.

"Take pity on me, Tsarevich Ivan," said the pike. "Throw me back into the blue sea!"

So Tsarevich Ivan threw the pike into the sea and walked on along the shore. Whether a long time passed by or a little time no one knows, but by and by the ball of thread rolled into a forest, and in the forest stood a little hut on chicken's feet, spinning round and round.

"Little hut, little hut, stand as once you stood, with your face to me and your back to the wood," said Tsarevich Ivan.

The hut turned its face to him and its back to the forest, and Tsarevich Ivan entered, and there, on the edge of the stove ledge, lay Baba-Yaga the Witch with the Switch, in a pose she liked best, her crooked nose to the ceiling pressed.

"What brings you here, good youth?" asked Baba-Yaga. "Is there aught you come to seek? Come, good youth, I pray you, speak!"

Said Tsarevich Ivan:

144

"First give me food and drink, you old hag, and steam me in the bath, and then ask your questions."

So Baba-Yaga steamed him in the bath, gave him food and drink and put him to bed, and then Tsarevich Ivan told her that he was seeking his wife, Vasilisa the Wise and Clever.

"I know where she is," said Baba-Yaga. "Koshchei the Deathless has her in his power. It will be hard getting her back, for it is not easy to get the better of Koshchei. His death is at the point of a needle, the needle is in an egg, the egg in a duck, the duck in a hare, the hare in a stone chest and the chest at the top of a tall oak-tree which Koshchei the Deathless guards as the apple of his own eye."

Tsarevich Ivan spent the night in Baba-Yaga's hut, and in the morning she told him where the tall oak-tree was to be found. Whether he was long on the way or not no one knows, but by and by he came

to the tall oak-tree. It stood there and it rustled and swayed, and the stone chest was at the top of it and very hard to reach.

All of a sudden, lo and behold!—the bear came running and it pulled out the oak-tree, roots and all. Down fell the chest, and it broke open. Out of the chest bounded a hare and away it tore as fast as it could. But another hare appeared and gave it chase. It caught up the first hare and tore it to bits. Out of the hare flew a duck, and it soared up to the very sky. But in a trice the drake was upon it and it struck the duck so hard that it dropped the egg, and down the egg fell into the blue sea.

At this Tsarevich Ivan began weeping bitter tears, for how could he find the egg in the sea! But all at once the pike came swimming to the shore with the egg in its mouth. Tsarevich Ivan cracked the egg, took out the needle and began trying to break off the point. The more he bent it, the more Koshchei the Deathless writhed and twisted. But all in vain. For Tsarevich Ivan broke off the point of the needle, and Koshchei fell down dead.

Tsarevich Ivan then went to Koshchei's palace of white stone. And Vasilisa the Wise and Clever ran out to him and kissed him on his honey-sweet mouth. And Tsarevich Ivan and Vasilisa the Wise and Clever went back to their own home and lived together long and happily till they were quite, quite old.

Wee Little Havroshechka

There are good people in the world and some who are not so good. There are also people who are shameless in their wickedness.

Wee Little Havroshechka had the bad luck to fall in with such as these. She was an orphan and these people took her in and brought her up only to make her work till she could not stand. She spun and wove and did the housework and had to answer for everything.

Now, the mistress of the house had three daughters. The eldest was called One-Eye, the second Two-Eyes, and the youngest Three-Eyes.

The three sisters did nothing all day but sit by the gate and watch what went on in the street, while Wee Little Havroshechka sewed, spun and wove for them and never heard a kind word in return.

Sometimes Wee Little Havroshechka would got out into the field, put her arms round the neck of her brindled cow and pour out all her sorrows to her.

"Brindled, my dear," she would say. "They beat me and scold me, they don't give me enough to eat, and yet they forbid me to cry. I am to have five poods of flax spun, woven, bleached and rolled by to-morrow."

And the cow would say in reply:

"My bonny lass, you have only to climb into one of my ears and come out through the other, and your work will be done for you."

And just as Brindled said, so it was. Wee Little Havroshechka would climb into one of the cow's ears, and come out through the other. And, lo and behold! there lay the cloth, all woven and bleached and rolled.

Wee Little Havroshechka would then take the rolls of cloth to her mistress who would look at them and grunt and put them away in a chest and give Wee Little Havroshechka even more work to do.

And Wee Little Havroshechka would go to Brindled, put her arms round her and stroke her, climb into one of her ears and come out through the other, pick up the ready cloth and take it to her mistress again.

One day the old woman called her daughter One-Eye to her and said:

"My good child, my bonny child, go and see who helps the orphan with her work. Find out who spins the flax and who weaves the cloth and rolls it."

One-Eye went with Wee Little Havroshechka into the woods and she went with her into the fields, but she forgot her mother's command and she lay down on the grass and basked in the sun. And Wee Little Havroshechka murmured:

"Sleep, little eye, sleep!"

One-Eye shut her eye and fell asleep. While she slept, Brindled wove, bleached and rolled the cloth.

The mistress learned nothing, so she sent for Two-Eyes, her second daughter, and said to her:

"My good child, my bonny child, go and see who helps the orphan with her work."

Two-Eyes went with Wee Little Havroshechka, but she forgot her mother's command and she lay down on the grass and basked in the sun. And Wee Little Havroshechka murmured:

"Sleep, little eye! Sleep, the other little eye!"

Two-Eyes shut her eyes and dozed off. While she slept, Brindled wove, bleached and rolled the cloth.

The old woman was very angry and on the third day she told Three-Eyes, her third daughter, to go with Wee Little Havroshechka to whom she gave more work to do than ever.

Three-Eyes played and skipped about in the sun until she was so tired that she lay down on the grass. And Wee Little Havroshechka sang out:

"Sleep, little eye! Sleep, the other little eye!"

But she forgot all about the third little eye.

Two of Three-Eyes' eyes fell asleep, but the third looked on and saw everything. It saw Wee Little Havroshechka climb into one of the cow's ears and come out through the other and pick up the ready cloth.

Three-Eyes came home and she told her mother what she had seen. The old woman was overjoyed, and on the very next day she went to her husband and said:

"Go and kill the brindled cow."

The old man was astonished and tried to reason with her.

"Have you lost your wits, old woman?" he said. "The cow is a good one and still young."

"Kill it and say no more," the wife insisted.

There was no help for it and the old man began to sharpen his knife.

Wee Little Havroshechka found out about it and she ran to the field and threw her arms round Brindled.

"Brindled, my dear," she said, "they want to kill you!"

And the cow replied:

"Do not grieve, my bonny lass, and do what I tell you. Take my bones, tie them up in a kerchief, bury them in the garden and water them every day. Do not eat of my flesh and never forget me."

149

The old man killed the cow, and Wee Little Havroshechka did as
Brindled had told her to. She went hungry, but she would not touch
the meat, and she buried the bones in the garden and watered them
every day.

After a while an apple-tree grew up out of them, and a wonderful
tree it was! Its apples were round and juicy, its swaying boughs were
of silver and its rustling leaves were of gold. Whoever drove by would
stop to look and whoever came near marvelled.

A long time passed by and a little time, and one day One-Eye,
Two-Eyes and Three-Eyes were out walking in the garden. And who
should chance to be riding by at the time but a young man, handsome
and curly-haired and strong and rich. When he saw the juicy apples
he stopped and said to the girls teasingly:

"Fair maidens! Her will I marry amongst you three who brings me an apple off yonder tree."

And off rushed the sisters to the apple-tree, each trying to get ahead of the others.

But the apples which had been hanging very low and seemed within easy reach, now swung up high in the air above the sisters' heads.

The sisters tried to knock them down, but the leaves came down in a shower and blinded them. They tried to pluck the apples off, but the boughs caught in their braids and unplaited them. Struggle and stretch as they would, they could not reach the apples and only scratched their hands.

Then Wee Little Havroshechka walked up to the tree, and at once the boughs bent down and the apples came into her hands. She gave an apple to the handsome young stranger, and soon after that he married her. From that day on she knew no sorrow, but lived with her husband in health and cheer and grew richer from year to year.

Marya Morevna the Lovely Tsarevna

In a certain tsardom, in a certain realm, there once lived the son of a Tsar, Tsarevich Ivan by name, and his three sisters. The first was called Tsarevna Marya, the second, Tsarevna Olga, and the third, Tsarevna Anna.

Their mother and father were dead. On their deathbed they said to their son:

"Do not keep your sisters long unwed, but marry them off to whoever comes to woo them first."

Tsarevich Ivan buried his parents and, to try and wear off his sorrow, he went with his sisters for a walk in their green garden.

All of a sudden a black cloud came over the sky. A terrible storm was about to break.

"Come, sisters, let us go home," said Tsarevich Ivan.

No sooner had they reached the palace than the thunder crashed, the ceiling was rent in two, and a Falcon flew into the chamber. He struck against the floor, turned into a tall and handsome youth, and said:

"Good morrow to you, Tsarevich Ivan. Many is the time I came to your house as a guest, but now I am here as a wooer. For I wish to ask for the hand of your sister, Tsarevna Marya, in marriage."

"If my sister likes you, well and good, for I'll not force her will. She can marry you if so she chooses."

And Tsarevna Marya being willing, the Falcon married her and carried her off to his tsardom.

Day followed day, and hour followed hour, and a whole year went by before ever they knew it. Tsarevich Ivan and his two sisters went for a walk in the green garden, and again a black cloud covered the sky, the lightning flared, and a fierce wind began to blow.

"Come, sisters, let us go home," said Tsarevich Ivan.

No sooner had they reached the palace than the thunder crashed, the roof caved in, the ceiling was rent in two, and an Eagle came flying in. He struck against the floor and he turned into a tall and handsome youth.

"Good morrow, Tsarevich Ivan," said he. "Many is the time I came here as a guest, but now I come as a wooer."

And he asked for the hand of Tsarevna Olga in marriage.

Said Tsarevich Ivan:

"If Tsarevna Olga likes you, you can have her. For I would not force her will."

Tsarevna Olga gave her consent and married the Eagle. And the Eagle caught her up and carried her off to his tsardom.

Another year passed by and Tsarevich Ivan said to his youngest sister:

"Come, sister, let us take a walk in the green garden."

They walked a little while, and again a black cloud covered the sky, the lightning flared, and a fierce wind began to blow.

"Let us go home, sister!" said Tsarevich Ivan.

They came home, and before they had had time to sit down, the thunder crashed, the ceiling was rent in two, and a Raven came flying in. He struck against the floor and turned into a tall and handsome

154

youth. The other two were likely young men enough, but this one was even more so.

"Many is the time I came here as a guest, but now I come as a wooer," said the Raven. "Let me have Tsarevna Anna in marriage."

"My sister is free to do as she wills. If she likes you, she can marry you."

So Tsarevna Anna married the Raven, and he carried her off to his tsardom. Tsarevich Ivan was left all by himself. He lived alone for a whole year, and he missed his sisters very much.

"I think I shall go and look for my sisters," said he.

He made ready and set off on his journey. He rode and he rode, and by and by he came to a field where a whole host of warriors lay routed and dead.

"If there is a man left alive among you, let him answer me!" Tsarevich Ivan called out. "For I wish to know who it was that vanquished this mighty host."

And the only living man there replied:

"This whole mighty host was vanquished by Marya Morevna the Lovely Tsarevna."

Tsarevich Ivan rode on, and after a while he came upon a number of white tents set up in a field, and there, coming out to meet him, was Marya Morevna the Lovely Tsarevna.

"Good morrow, Tsarevich," said she. "Whither are you bound? Do you come of your own free will or on another's errand?"

Said Tsarevich Ivan in reply:

"Hale and hearty young men like myself never go anywhere but of their own free will."

"Well, if you are in no great haste, then be my guest and bide in my tent a while."

This Tsarevich Ivan was pleased to do. For two days and two nights he was Marya Morevna's guest, and so well did they like one another that they decided to marry then and there. Thus it was that Tsarevich Ivan and Marya Morevna the Lovely Tsarevna became man and wife, and he went with her to her far-off tsardom.

They lived together for a time till one day Marya Morevna bethought her of setting out again for the wars. She left her palace and everything in it in the care of Tsarevich Ivan and, pointing out a room to him the door of which was locked fast, said:

"Go all over and look after everything, but mind you never look into this one room."

But Tsarevich Ivan's curiosity got the better of him and, as soon as Marya Morevna had left, he hurried to the room and opened the door. He looked in, and what did he see but Koshchei the Deathless hanging there, chained to the wall with twelve chains.

Said Koshchei the Deathless in pleading tones:

"Take pity on me, Tsarevich Ivan, and give me some water to drink. For ten years have I been held here and such have been my torments as cannot be described. I have had no food and nothing to drink, and my throat is all dry and parched."

Tsarevich Ivan gave him a whole pailful of water to drink, and he drank it down and began to plead for more.

"One pail is not enough, I am still thirsty, so do let me have another," he begged.

Tsarevich Ivan gave him a second pail of water, and Koshchei gulped it down and asked for a third. But when he had finished his third pailful he got back all of his former strength, and he shook his chains and broke all the twelve of them.

"Thank you, Tsarevich Ivan," said Koshchei the Deathless. "Now you will never see Marya Morevna, no more than you can see your own ears."

And he flew out the window as swiftly as a whirlwind, caught up Marya Morevna the Lovely Tsarevna on the road and carried her off with him.

Tsarevich Ivan wept long and bitterly, and then he made ready and set off in search of Marya Morevna.

"Come what may, I shall find her!" said he.

A day passed by, and a second, and at dawn on the third day Tsarevich Ivan saw a beautiful palace before him. Beside the palace there grew an oak, and on its bough there perched a Falcon. The Falcon flew off the oak, struck against the ground and turned into a handsome youth.

"Ah, my own dear brother-in-law, I am indeed glad to see you!" he cried.

Hearing him, Tsarevna Marya ran out to meet her brother. She welcomed him joyously, asked after his health and began to tell him how she lived and fared. Tsarevich Ivan spent three days with them and then he said:

"I cannot stay with you longer. I am seeking my wife, Marya Morevna the Lovely Tsarevna."

"It won't be easy to find her," the Falcon told him. "Leave your silver spoon here just in case. We shall look at it and think of you."

Tsarevich Ivan left his silver spoon with the Falcon, and he set off

157

on his journey. He rode for a day, he rode for another day, and at dawn on the third day he saw a palace which was even more beautiful than the Falcon's. Beside the palace there grew an oak, and on its bough there perched an Eagle.

The Eagle flew off the tree, struck against the ground and, turning into a handsome youth, cried:

"Come, Tsarevna Olga, get up, for our own dear brother is here!"

Hearing him, Tsarevna Olga came running out of the palace. She began to kiss and embrace Tsarevich Ivan, to ask after his health and to tell him how she lived and fared. Tsarevich Ivan spent three days with them and then he said:

"I cannot bide with you longer. I am seeking my wife, Marya Morevna the Lovely Tsarevna."

Said the Eagle:

"It will not be easy to find her. Leave your silver fork with us. We shall look at it and think of you."

So Tsarevich Ivan left his silver fork with them and went on his way.

He rode for a day, he rode for another day, and at dawn on the third day he saw a palace which far surpassed the first two in beauty and splendour. Beside the palace there grew an oak, and on its bough there perched a Raven.

The Raven flew off the oak, struck against the ground and, turning into a handsome youth, cried:

"Tsarevna Anna, make haste and come, our own dear brother is here!"

Hearing him, Tsarevna Anna came running out of the palace. She welcomed Tsarevich Ivan joyously, kissed and embraced him, asked after his health and began to tell him how she lived and fared.

Tsarevich Ivan spent three days with them, and then he said:

"I must bid you good-bye, for I am off to seek my wife, Marya Morevna the Lovely Tsarevna."

Said the Raven in reply:

"It will not be easy to find her. Leave your silver snuff-box with us. We shall look at it and think of you."

Tsarevich Ivan gave him his silver snuff-box and, taking leave of them both, went on his way.

A day passed by, and another and, on the third day, Tsarevich Ivan finally found his beloved.

When she saw him, Marya Morevna threw her arms around Tsarevich Ivan, burst into tears and said:

"Ah, Tsarevich Ivan, why did you not listen to me, but opened the room where Koshchei the Deathless was kept and let him out?"

"Forgive me, Marya Morevna, and let bygones be bygones. Come away with me while Koshchei the Deathless is nowhere to be seen and, perhaps, he will not overtake us."

So they made ready and rode away together.

And Koshchei the Deathless was out hunting. It was evening by the time he turned his way homewards, and his goodly horse stumbled under him.

"Why do you stumble, you old bag of bones?" he asked. "Is it that you sense some misfortune?"

Said the horse in reply:

"Tsarevich Ivan came, and he carried off Marya Morevna."

"Can we catch them up?"

"If we were to sow some wheat, wait till it ripened, reap and thresh it and grind it into flour, bake five ovenfuls of bread, and not go after them till we had eaten it all up, we should still catch them up."

So Koshchei the Deathless sent his horse into a gallop, and he caught up Tsarevich Ivan.

"I'll forgive you this first time," said he, "for you were kind to me, you gave me water to drink, and I'll forgive you a second time, but if you dare to go against me a third time, then I'll hack you to pieces."

And he took Marya Morevna from him and rode away with her, and Tsarevich Ivan sat down on a stone by the side of the road and

159

began to cry. He wept and he sobbed, and then he went back again for Marya Morevna. And Koshchei the Deathless happened to be away from home as before.

"Come with me, Marya Morevna," said Tsarevich Ivan.

"Ah, Tsarevich Ivan, he will overtake us again!"

"Let him. We shall at least have spent an hour or two together!"

So they made ready and rode away.

By and by Koshchei the Deathless turned his way homewards, and his goodly horse stumbled under him.

"You old bag of bones you, why do you stumble? Is it that you sense some misfortune?" asked he.

"Tsarevich Ivan came, and he carried Marya Morevna off with him."

"Can we catch them up?"

"If we were to sow some barley, wait till it ripened, reap and thresh it, brew beer out of it, drink till we were drunk and not go after them till we had slept it off, we should still catch them up."

So Koshchei the Deathless put his horse into a gallop, and he caught up Tsarevich Ivan.

"I told you you would no more see Marya Morevna than your own ears," said he.

And he took her away from Tsarevich Ivan and carried her off with him.

Tsarevich Ivan was left alone, he wept and he cried, and then he went back again for Marya Morevna. And Koshchei the Deathless happened to be away as before.

"Come with me, Marya Morevna," said Tsarevich Ivan.

"Ah, Tsarevich Ivan, he will overtake us and hack you to pieces!"

"Let him! I cannot live without you."

So they made ready and rode away. By and by Koshchei the Deathless turned his way homewards, and his goodly horse stumbled under him.

"Why do you stumble? Is it that you sense some misfortune?" he asked.

"Tsarevich Ivan came, and he took Marya Morevna away."

So Koshchei galloped after Tsarevich Ivan and, when he had caught him up, he hacked him to pieces. He put the pieces in a tarred barrel, bound the barrel with iron hoops and threw it in the blue sea. And he carried Marya Morevna off with him again.

Now at this selfsame time the silver things Tsarevich Ivan had left with his brothers-in-law turned dark and tarnished.

161

"Oh," said the brothers-in-law, "Tsarevich Ivan must have met with some misfortune."

So the Eagle swooped down on to the blue sea, seized the barrel and carried it out on to the shore.

The Falcon flew after living water, and the Raven flew after dead water, and the two of them came flying back to where the Eagle was waiting for them. They broke up the barrel, took out the pieces into which Tsarevich Ivan's body had been hacked, washed them and put them all together properly.

The Raven sprayed the pieces with dead water, and they grew fast to one another, and then the Falcon sprayed them with living water, and Tsarevich Ivan rose with a start and said:

"Ah, what a long sleep I have had!"

"You would have slept longer if it were not for us," his brothers-in-law replied. "And now come and be our guest."

"No, my brothers, I must go to seek Marya Morevna."

d off he went.

He found Marya Morevna and said to her:

"Ask Koshchei the Deathless where it was he got himself such a fine horse."

And Marya Morevna bided her chance and then she asked Koshchei the Deathless about his horse.

Said Koshchei the Deathless:

"Beyond the Thrice-Nine Lands, in the Thrice-Ten Tsardom there lives Baba-Yaga the Witch. She lives in the forest beyond the Flaming River, and she has a mare on which she flies round the world every day. She has other fine mares too. I tended them for three days, and I let not a single mare run off, so Baba-Yaga gave me a colt in reward for my services."

"How did you manage to cross the Flaming River?"

"With the help of my magic kerchief. I have only to wave it thrice to the right of me, and a very tall bridge will rise up that the flames cannot reach."

Marya Morevna heard him out and she passed on every word to Tsarevich Ivan. And she carried off Koshchei's magic kerchief too and gave it to him.

Tsarevich Ivan crossed the Flaming River and made for Baba-Yaga's house. He walked for a long, long time without food or drink, and then he came upon a strange bird and her brood.

Said Tsarevich Ivan:

"I think I shall eat one of the chicks."

"Do not touch my chicks, Tsarevich Ivan," said the bird in pleading tones. "Who knows but you might have need of me some day!"

Tsarevich Ivan walked on and, by and by, he came upon a beehive in the forest.

"I think I shall take some honey," said he.

But the bee queen began to plead with him and said:

"Do not touch my honey, Tsarevich Ivan. Who knows but you might have need of me some day!"

Tsarevich Ivan did not touch the honey, but walked on.

By and by he came upon a lioness and her cub.

Said Tsarevich Ivan:

"I think I shall at least eat up that lion cub there. I am so hungry that I can hardly stand on my legs."

"Do not touch my cub," said the lioness in pleading tones. "Who knows but you might have need of me some day!"

"Very well, let it be as you ask."

And he walked on, as hungry as ever. He walked and he walked, and by and by he came to Baba-Yaga's house. There were twelve poles round the house, and human heads were stuck on eleven of them, while the twelfth was bare.

"Good morrow, Grandma!" said Tsarevich Ivan to Baba-Yaga.

"Good morrow to you, Tsarevich Ivan. What brings you here? Do you come because it pleases you or is it that you have need of me?"

163

"I come to offer you my services and to earn one of your fine steeds in reward."

"Very well, Tsarevich Ivan. It is not for a year, but for only three days that you must serve me. If you keep my mares safe, you shall have one of my fine steeds. If you don't, then your head will crown the last pole of the twelve, and you'll only have yourself to blame."

They struck a bargain, and Baba-Yaga gave Tsarevich Ivan food and drink and told him to set to work. No sooner had Tsarevich Ivan driven the mares to pasture than they lifted their tails and ran off every which way across the meadows, and before he could raise his eyes to see where they went they were gone out of sight. Tsarevich Ivan sorrowed and wept, and then he sat down on a stone and fell asleep.

The sun was setting when the strange bird came flying up.

"Wake up, Tsarevich Ivan," said she. "The mares are all back in their stalls."

Tsarevich Ivan rose and went home, and Baba-Yaga made a great to-do and she shouted at her mares and scolded them.

"Why did you come back home?" she demanded of them.

"What else could we do? The birds came flying from all over the earth and they nearly plucked out our eyes."

"Well, don't run over the meadows tomorrow, but scatter in the dense forests."

Tsarevich Ivan slept the night through and, in the morning, Baba-Yaga said to him:

"Take care, Tsarevich Ivan. If you do not keep my mares safe but lose a single one of them, your head will crown the pole."

Tsarevich Ivan drove the mares out to pasture, and they at once lifted their tails and ran off into the dense forests. And Tsarevich Ivan sat down on a stone, he wept and he cried, and he fell asleep. The sun had already sunk beyond the forest when the lioness came running.

"Wake up, Tsarevich Ivan," said she. "All the mares are back in their stalls."

Tsarevich Ivan got up and went home. And Baba-Yaga made a

great to-do, she shouted at her mares and scolded them harder than ever.

"Why did you come back home?" she demanded of them.

"What else could we do? The fiercest beasts from all over the earth came running, and they very nearly tore us to shreds!"

"Well, run and hide in the blue sea tomorrow."

Tsarevich Ivan slept the night through and, in the morning, Baba-Yaga sent him off to pasture her mares again.

"If you don't keep them safe, your head will crown the pole," said she.

Tsarevich Ivan drove the mares to pasture in the field, and at once they lifted their tails and vanished from sight. Into the blue sea they ran, and they stood up to their necks in the water.

Tsarevich Ivan sat down on a stone, he wept and he cried, and he fell asleep.

The sun sank beyond the forest, and the bee came flying up and said:

"Wake up, Tsarevich Ivan, all the mares are back in their stalls. Only mind, when you get back to her house, do not show yourself to Baba-Yaga, but go to the stable and hide behind the crib. There is a mangy colt there wallowing in the dung. Take him, and in the deep of night leave the house."

Tsarevich Ivan rose, he stole into the stable and lay down behind the crib. And all the while Baba-Yaga was shouting at the top of her voice and berating her mares.

"Why did you come back?" she demanded of them.

"What else could we do? Swarms of bees came flying from every corner of the earth and they stung us all over till the blood showed."

Baba-Yaga went to bed and fell asleep and, on the stroke of midnight, Tsarevich Ivan saddled her mangiest colt and rode to the Flaming River. When he reached the river he waved his magic kerchief thrice to the right of him and, lo and behold! there before him was a fine, tall bridge spanning the river.

165

Tsarevich Ivan rode across and waved his kerchief twice to the left of him and instead of the fine, tall bridge there appeared a poor, low, narrow one.

In the morning Baba-Yaga woke up and, seeing that her mangy colt was gone, she rushed off in pursuit. Like the wind she went in her iron mortar, using her pestle for a whip and sweeping the tracks away with her broom.

She flew to the Flaming River, took one look and said to herself:

"A bridge. Just what I need!"

And she started off across the bridge. But just when she had reached its very middle, the bridge broke down under her, and Baba-Yaga fell in the river. And so that was how she met her end, and a cruel end it was.

And Tsarevich Ivan pastured his colt in the lush, green meadows, and the colt grew into a strong and handsome steed.

Then Tsarevich Ivan rode to the house of Koshchei the Deathless, and out ran Marya Morevna the Lovely Tsarevna and she threw her arms around his neck.

"How ever did you manage to escape death?" she asked him.

And nothing would do but he must tell her all about it.

"And now you must come away with me," said Tsarevich Ivan.

"I'm afraid, Tsarevich Ivan! If Koshchei overtakes us, he'll chop you to pieces again!"

"He'll not catch us up this time. For I have a fine, strong steed that flies like the wind."

And they mounted the steed and rode away.

167

By and by Koshchei the Deathless turned his way homewards, and his horse stumbled under him.

"Why do you stumble, you old bag of bones?" he asked him.

"Tsarevich Ivan came, and he carried off Marya Morevna," the horse replied.

"Can we catch them up?"

"I cannot say, for now Tsarevich Ivan has a horse as fine as I am, or better."

"I shan't let it rest at that," said Koshchei the Deathless. "I'll go after them!"

Whether a long time passed by or a little time no one knows, but he caught up Tsarevich Ivan and, jumping to the ground, was about to pierce him with his sharp sword. But before he could do it, Tsarevich Ivan's horse struck him with his hoof with all his might and smashed his head, and Tsarevich Ivan finished him off with his cudgel.

After that Tsarevich Ivan piled up a heap of wood and made up a fire. He burnt up the body of Koshchei the Deathless, and he strewed his ashes in the wind.

Marya Morevna mounted Koshchei's horse, Tsarevich Ivan mounted his own, and away they rode. First, they went to see the Raven, then the Eagle and then the Falcon. And they were welcomed with joy by all three.

"Ah, Tsarevich Ivan, we had lost all hope of ever seeing you!" they all said. "But at least all your troubles have not been in vain. If you searched the world over you could not find a bride as lovely as Marya Morevna!"

Tsarevich Ivan and Marya Morevna feasted and made merry for a time, and then they went back to their own tsardom. And there they lived in health and in cheer for many a long and prosperous year, never knowing hunger or need, but drinking their fill of ale and mead.

Ivan—Young of Years, Old of Wisdom

nce upon a time there was an old man and his wife. The old man hunted game and wild fowl, and that was all they had to live on. Many a year did they live, but were as poor as ever. The old woman sorrowed and grieved.

"What a wretched life we've had," she said time and again. "Never a good thing to eat or drink, never a fine dress to put on. And we've no children, either, no one to take care of us in our old age."

"Don't grieve, old woman," the old man soothed her. "While I've my two hands to work with and my two feet to carry me, we'll have enough to eat. And let tomorrow take care of itself."

So he said and went off to hunt.

All that day from morning till night the old man tramped about in the woods, but not a bird or a beast could he catch or kill. He did not like to go home empty-handed, but what could he do? The sun was setting, and it was time to turn homewards!

He had just started back, when there came a flapping of wings, and out of the bushes close by flew a bird of wondrous beauty.

But by the time he took aim, it was gone.

"It's a sorry hunter I am," sighed the old man. He peered under

the bush where the bird had been, and lo! there in a nest lay thirty-three eggs.

"Better that than nothing," said he.

He tightened his belt and, slipping all of the thirty-three eggs inside his *caftan*, went home.

On and on he walked, and his belt came loose and one by one the eggs began falling out.

Down fell an egg, and a lad hopped out of it, down fell another egg, and out hopped another lad. Thirty-two eggs fell out, and thirty-two lads hopped out of them.

But just then the old man pulled his belt tight, and one egg—the thirty-third—stayed where it was. The old man looked back, and he could not believe his eyes: thirty-two bonny lads followed in his steps, all of them of the same height and as alike as peas in a pod. And they all spoke out with one voice:

"Since you've found us you can take us home. You're our father now and we are your sons."

"What a lucky day for me and my old wife!" thought the old man. "Not a child in all these years, and now—thirty-two sons at one stroke."

They came home, and the old man said.

"Haven't you sighed and cried for children all these years, old woman? Well, here I've brought you thirty-two sons, all bonny lads, too. Now lay the table and feed them."

And he told her how he had found them.

The old woman stood there, and she could not say a word. Thus she stayed for a while, and then, drawing a deep breath, rushed to lay the table. Just then the old man undid his belt and was about to take off his *caftan* when down fell the thirty-third egg, and a thirty-third lad hopped out of it.

"Why, where do you come from?"

"I'm Ivan, your youngest son."

And the old man recalled that he had indeed found thirty-three eggs in the nest.

"All right, then, Ivan, sit down to supper."

No sooner had the thirty-three lads sat down to eat than they cleaned up all of the old woman's stores. But they got up from the table neither hungry nor full.

They slept the night through, and on the following morning Ivan said:

"You've found yourself sons, Father, now give us some work to do."

"What kind of work can I give you, lads? My old woman and I, we've never ploughed nor sowed in our life, for we've never had a horse or a plough."

"Well, if you haven't you haven't, and it can't be helped," said Ivan. "We'll have to go to other folk to find work. Now go to the blacksmith, Father, and have him make us thirty-three scythes."

Now while the old man was away at the smithy having the scythes forged, Ivan and his brothers made thirty-three scythe-handles and thirty-three rakes.

When the father came back from the smithy, Ivan dealt out the tools and said:

"Come, brothers, let's find us some work to do and earn enough money to start life on our own and take care of our old mother and father."

The brothers said good-bye to their mother and father and set off.

Whether they were on their way for a long or a little time nobody knows, but at last they saw a big town. And out of that town the Tsar's Steward came riding. He rode up to them and asked:

"Ho, my lads, where are you going—to or from work? If it's to work, follow me, for I have something for you to do."

"And what is that?"

"Nothing very hard," replied the Steward. "You will have to mow the grass in the Tsar's own meadows, and then dry the hay, gather it in cocks an stack it. Who is the leader among you?"

Nobody answered, so Ivan stepped forward and said:

"Take us there and show us around."

The Steward led them to the Tsar's own meadows.

"Will three weeks be enough for you?" he asked.

"If the weather keeps up, three days will be enough," Ivan replied.

The Tsar's Steward was greatly pleased.

"Then fall to, my lads," he said, "and don't worry about food and pay; all that you need you will get."

Said Ivan:

"Roast us thirty-three bulls and stand us thirty-three pails of wine and give us a *kalach* apiece. That's all we'll need."

Off rode the Tsar's Steward. The brothers sharpened their scythes and plied them so heartily that they whistled as they cut the air. The work went on briskly, and by evening all the grass was mowed. Meanwhile the Tsar's kitchen had sent up the fare: thirty-three roast bulls, thirty-three pails of wine and a *kalach* apiece. The brothers each ate half a bull and drank half a pail of wine and took half a *kalach*, and then they all tumbled down to sleep.

The next day, when the sun grew warm, the brothers made the hay and gathered it in cocks and by evening had it all stacked. And again they each ate half a bull with half a *kalach* and drank half a pail of wine. After that Ivan sent one of his brothers to the Tsar's courtyard.

"Tell them to come and see how we've done our work," said he.

The brothers came back with the Steward, and soon after the Tsar himself followed. The Tsar counted all the haystacks and he walked all over his meadows—not a blade of grass could he find left standing.

"You've made the hay well and in good time, my lads," said he. "For this you have my praises and, over and above, here is a hundred

173

rubles and a forty-pail barrel of wine. But now there is one more task I would have you do. The hay must be guarded. Somebody has been coming and eating it up every year, and we can't find even trace of the thief."

And Ivan replied:

"Let my brothers go home, Your Majesty, I shall guard the hay alone."

To this the Tsar agreed, and so Ivan's thirty-two brothers went to the Tsar's palace and got their money as well as a sound supper and a good drink of wine. And after that they set off homewards.

And Ivan went back to the Tsar's meadows. At night he stayed awake and guarded the Tsar's hay, while by day he ate and drank and took his rest in the Tsar's kitchen.

Autumn came, and the nights grew long and dark. One evening Ivan climbed to the top of a haystack, burrowed into the hay and lay there, wide awake. At the stroke of midnight it suddenly grew light as day, as if the sun had risen. Ivan peered out and what should he see but a Mare with a Golden Mane. Out of the sea she sprang and dashed straight up to his haystack. The earth shook under her hoofs, her golden mane streamed in the wind, her nostrils spurted flame, and clouds of smoke poured from her ears.

Up she ran to the haystack and began eating the hay. And Ivan caught his chance and leaped on her back. The Mare left the stack and away she raced across the Tsar's own meadows. But Ivan held on to her mane with his left hand, and he gripped a leathern whip in his right. And he whipped the Mare with the Golden Mane and drove her straight into the moors and mosses.

The Mare galloped over the moors and mosses for a long time, till at last she sank to her belly in the mire. She stopped then and she spoke these words:

"You were quick enough to catch me, Ivan, and to keep your seat on me, and clever enough to tame me as well. Don't beat or hurt me any more, and I shall be your faithful servant."

So off he led her to the Tsar's courtyard and locked her up in a stable, and himself went to the Tsar's kitchen and tumbled down to sleep. In the morning he came to the Tsar and said:

"I have found out who stole the hay from your meadows, Your Majesty, and I've caught the thief too. Come, let's have a look at him."

When the Tsar saw the Mare with the Golden Mane he was greatly pleased.

"Well, Ivan," he said, "you may be young of years, but you are old of wisdom. For your faithful service I make you my Chief Groom."

And from that time Ivan was called Ivan—Young of Years, Old of Wisdom.

Ivan took up his duties at the Tsar's stables, and he didn't sleep nights looking after the Tsar's horses who daily grew more smooth and sleek. Their coats became glossy as silk and their manes and tails were always well combed and fluffy—a pleasant sight, indeed.

The Tsar was delighted and could not find enough words to praise Ivan.

"Well done, Ivan—Young of Years, Old of Wisdom! I've never yet had so fine a groom."

But the old stablemen envied him and said:

"To be ordered about by a village bumpkin! A fine Chief Groom for the Tsar's stables!"

And they started plotting mischief against him. But Ivan went about his work and had not an inkling of the danger that hung over him.

At that time an old drunkard, a tavern frequenter, came wandering into the Tsar's stable-yard.

"Give me a drop, lads, to cure that headache I caught last night," said he. "If you do, I'll set you on the right way to get rid of the Chief Groom."

The stablemen were overjoyed and gave him a glass of wine.

The old drunkard emptied the glass and said:

"The Tsar is dying to have the Self-Playing Psaltry, the Dancing Goose and the Glee-Maker Cat. Many fine lads set out on their own, and still more were sent after those wonders, but never a one came back. Now you go to the Tsar and say that Ivan—Young of Years, Old of Wisdom has boasted that he can get them, with no trouble at all. The Tsar will send him off, and he will never come back again."

The stablemen thanked the old drunkard, gave him a second glass of wine and went straight to the front porch of the Tsar's palace. They stood there gossiping under the Tsar's windows, and the Tsar caught sight of them, came out of his palace and asked:

"What are you talking about, my lads? What do you want?"

"Well, Your Majesty, it's just that Ivan—Young of Years, Old of

Wisdom has boasted that he can get the Self-Playing Psaltery, the Dancing Goose and the Glee-Maker Cat. That is why we stand arguing here; some say he can fetch them, and others say he can't, that it's just empty words."

When the Tsar heard such speeches, his face changed and his hands shook.

"Ah," thought he, "if only I could get hold of those wonders! All the other tsars would envy me. I've sent so many men for them, and never a one came back!"

And he straightaway sent for his Chief Groom.

As soon as Ivan came in, the Tsar shouted:

"Waste no time, Ivan, but go at once and fetch me the Self-Playing Psaltery, the Dancing Goose and the Glee-Maker Cat."

And Ivan—Young of Years, Old of Wisdom replied:

"Goodness me, I've never even heard of them, Your Majesty! Where do you want me to go?"

But the Tsar flew into a rage and stamped his foot.

"What's all this talk about? Would you disobey your Tsar's orders? Off you go at once. If you fetch me what I ask, I shall reward you; if not, I'll out with my sword and off with your head!"

Ivan—Young of Years, Old of Wisdom left the Tsar with a heavy heart and a drooping head. He began saddling his Mare with the Golden Mane, and the Mare asked him:

"Why so unhappy, Master, is there anything amiss?"

"How can I be happy when the Tsar has ordered me to fetch him the Self-Playing Psaltery, the Dancing Goose and the Glee-Maker Cat, and I haven't even heard of them."

"Oh, well, that isn't anything to worry about," said the Mare with the Golden Mane. "Get on my back and let us go to the old witch Baba-Yaga and ask her where to find those marvels."

So Ivan—Young of Years, Old of Wisdom got ready for the journey and mounted Golden Mane. And that was the last people saw of him. No one saw him pass through the gates—he was too quick for that.

Whether he went far or near and whether he was long on his way or not nobody knows, but at last he rode into a dense forest. It was very dark there, not a ray of light filtering through. The Mare with the Golden Mane grew lean with weariness and Ivan—Young of Years, Old of Wisdom felt tired and worn. But at last they reached a glade in the woods and saw a little hut on a hen's foot with a spindle for a heel. It kept turning round and round from west to east, and Ivan—Young of Years, Old of Wisdom rode up and said:

"Little hut, little hut, turn your back to the trees and your face to me, please. Not for years will I stay, but to sleep till day."

The hut turned its face to him, and Ivan tied his Mare to a pole, ran up on to the porch and pushed the door ajar.

And who should he see there but Baba-Yaga, the witch with the switch, a bony hag with a nose like a snag, her pestle and mortar beside her.

Baba-Yaga caught sight of her guest and croaked:

"Ugh, ugh, Russian blood, never met by me before, now I smell it at my door. Who comes here? Where from? Where to?"

"Is it so you treat a guest, Granny? Bothering him with talk when he's hungry and cold! At home in Rus they'd first let a wayfarer eat and drink and get warm, and give him a rest and a bath, and then start asking questions."

Baba-Yaga felt shamed and discomfited. "Don't be cross with an old woman, my fine lad," cried she. "We're not in Rus, you know. But I'll soon put things to rights."

And she flew about setting the table with food and drink. She made her guest welcome, and then she ran out to heat the stove in the bath-house. Ivan—Young of Years, Old of Wisdom steamed and bathed himself, and Baba-Yaga made up his bed and put him down to rest. Then she sat down at his bedside and asked:

"Tell me where lies your way, lad? Have you come here of your own free will, or has anyone's ill-will driven you?"

"The Tsar sent me to fetch him the Self-Playing Psaltery, the Dancing Goose and the Glee-Maker Cat," Ivan replied. "And I'd be ever so thankful, Granny, if you told me where to find them."

"I know where they are, my lad, but they're hard to get. Many a fine lad has gone after them, but never a one came back."

"Well, Granny, what is to be, will be, so you had better help me in my need and tell me where to go."

"Ah, well, my good lad, I pity you sore, but I see there is nothing to do but to help you. Leave your Mare with the Golden Mane here, she will be safe with me, and take this ball of yarn, and tomorrow, when you go out, drop it on the ground and follow wherever it rolls. It will bring you to my middle sister. Show her the ball and she will help you in all she can and tell you all she knows. And then she will send you on to our eldest sister."

On the following day Baby-Yaga woke up her guest before dawn, and she gave him food and drink and saw him out into the yard. And Ivan—Young of Years, Old of Wisdom thanked her, took his leave and set out on his way. A tale is short a-telling and long a-doing, but the ball of yarn rolled on and on, and Ivan went after it.

A day passed, and another, and a third, and the ball of yarn rolled up to a little hut on a sparrow's foot with a spindle for a heel. Here it stopped, and Ivan—Young of Years, Old of Wisdom called out:

"Little hut, little hut, turn your back to the trees and your face to me, please."

The hut turned round, and Ivan went up on to the porch. He opened the door, and a gruff voice said:

"Ugh, ugh, Russian blood, never met by me before, now I smell it at my door. Who comes here? Where from? Where to?"

Ivan—Young of Years, Old of Wisdom showed Baba-Yaga the ball of yarn, and she cried out in wonder:

"Dear me, so you're not a stranger at all, but a welcome guest sent by my sister. Why didn't you say so at once?" And she flew about laying the table with dainties and drinks for her guest, and made him welcome.

"Eat and drink your fill," she said, "and lie down to rest. Then we'll talk about business."

So Ivan—Young of Years, Old of Wisdom ate and drank his fill and then he tumbled down to rest, while Baba-Yaga, the second witch-sister, sat down at his bedside and began asking him all about everything. And he told her who he was, whence he came, and whither he was going.

Said Baba-Yaga:

"The way is not far, but I don't know whether you'll get there and live. The Self-Playing Psaltery, the Dancing Goose and the Glee-Maker Cat all belong to our nephew Zmei Gorinich, the Dragon of the Mountains. Many a fine lad has gone there, and never a one came back, for they all fell prey to the Dragon. Now, he is the son of our eldest sister, and we'll have to ask her to help you, or you will not come back alive, either. I know what to do. I shall send her my messenger the Wise Raven to warn her. But now go to bed, for I shall wake you up early tomorrow."

Ivan—Young of Years, Old of Wisdom had a sound night's sleep, and early in the morning he rose, washed and ate what Baba-Yaga set before him. After that she gave him a ball of red wool and came out to show him the way, and here they said good-bye. The ball of wool began to roll, and Ivan—Young of Years, Old of Wisdom went after it.

On and on he walked from sunrise to sunset and from sunset to dawn. Whenever he grew weary he would take up the ball of wool and sit down for a rest and a bite to eat. He would eat a crust of bread and drink a drop of spring water, and then set off on his way again.

By the end of the third day the ball of wool stopped at a large house. The house was built on twelve stones and propped by twelve pillars, and it was surrounded by a tall paling.

181

A dog barked, and Baba-Yaga, the eldest witch-sister, ran out on the porch. She quietened the dog, and said:

"I know all about you, my bonny lad. My sister's messenger the Wise Raven has been here. I'll find a way to help you in your need. But come in and have some food and drink, you must be hungry and footsore."

And she showed him in and gave him food and drink.

"Now you must hide," said she. "My son Zmei Gorinich is coming soon. He is always very cross and hungry when he comes, so I fear he may gobble you up."

And opening a trap-door, she added:

"Go down into the cellar and sit there till I call you."

Scarcely had she closed the trap-door, when there came a terrible noise and clatter. The door burst open, and in flew Zmei Gorinich, making such a din that the very walls shook.

"I smell Russian flesh!" he roared.

"Oh, no, my son, how can that be! It's years since even a grey wolf came prowling here or a falcon flying. It is you yourself have been flying about the wide world and brought the smell with you."

And she bustled about, setting the table. She pulled a roast bull from the oven and she fetched a pail of wine from the pantry. And Zmei Gorinich drained the pail at a single draught and gobbled up the roast bull and became more cheerful.

"Ah, Mother, I wish I could have a bit of fun, play cards with someone or something."

"I could find you someone to play cards with and to have fun with, but I fear you will harm him."

"Then call him in, Mother, and have no fear. I won't harm anyone, for I'm dying for a game of cards, and a bit of fun."

"Well, son, mind that you keep your promise," Baba-Yaga replied and she went and lifted the trap-door.

"Come up, Ivan—Young of Years, Old of Wisdom, do your host a favour and play cards with him."

182

They sat down at the table, and Zmei Gorinich said:

"Let us play, and mind: the winner eats the loser."

All night they played, and Baba-Yaga helped Ivan, so that by morning he had won the game.

Said Zmei Gorinich in pleading tones:

"Stay with us a while more, my fine lad, that I may try and win my own back. We can have another game when I get home tonight."

He flew away, and Ivan—Young of Years, Old of Wisdom had a sound sleep, and a good meal to follow it.

At sundown Zmei Gorinich came back, and he ate another roast bull, drank a pail and a half of wine and said:

"Well, now let's sit down and play, and I'll try and win my own back."

They sat down to play, but Zmei Gorinich hadn't slept all that night and had flown about the world all day, so he soon became drowsy. And Ivan—Young of Years, Old of Wisdom won again with Baba-Yaga's help. Said Zmei Gorinich:

"Now I must fly off on business, but we shall have a third game in the evening."

Ivan—Young of Years, Old of Wisdom had a good rest and a sound sleep, and Zmei Gorinich had not slept for two nights and had flown all over the wide world, so he came home all tired out. He ate a roast bull and drank two pails of wine and he called to his guest:

"Sit down, my bonny lad, and I'll try and win my own back."

But he was so weary and drowsy that Ivan soon won for the third time.

Zmei Gorinich was very frightened, and he fell on his knees and he cried in pleading tones:

"Don't eat me up, don't kill me, Ivan—Young of Years, Old of Wisdom! I shall do you any service you like."

And then he fell on his knees before his mother and begged her too to persuade Ivan to spare him. And of course that was all Ivan wanted.

183

"Well, now, Zmei Gorinich," said he, "I've won three games of you, but if you give me your three wonders: the Self-Playing Psaltery, the Dancing Goose and the Glee-Maker Cat, we shall call it a bargain."

Zmei Gorinich laughed out with joy, and he set to hugging his guest and his old mother Baba-Yaga.

"You can have them, and welcome!" he cried. "I can get myself still better ones."

And Zmei Gorinich held a grand feast and he treated Ivan handsomely and called him brother. He even offered to carry him home.

"Why should you tramp on foot and carry the Self-Playing Psaltery, the Dancing Goose and the Glee-Maker Cat? I can take you wherever it is you want to go in a twinkling."

"That's right, son," said Baba-Yaga. "Take your guest to your aunt, my youngest sister. And don't forget to call on your other aunt on the way back. It's quite a time since they both saw you."

The feast came to an end, and Ivan—Young of Years, Old of Wisdom took his marvels and said good-bye to Baba-Yaga, and Zmei Gorinich caught him up and soared into the blue sky. Before an hour had passed they came down again beside the hut of the youngest of the three Baba-Yagas. And Baba-Yaga ran out on to the porch, and very glad she was to see them. Ivan—Young of Years, Old of Wisdom wasted no time but saddled his Mare with the Golden Mane and, taking leave of the youngest Baba-Yaga and her nephew Zmei Gorinich, started back to his own tsardom.

He came home and he brought all the three wonders with him safe and sound. And the Tsar was having guests just then: three tsars with their tsareviches, three kings with their princes, and ministers and boyars besides.

Ivan—Young of Years, Old of Wisdom came into the chamber and he gave the Tsar the Self-Playing Psaltery, the Dancing Goose and the Glee-Maker Cat. And wasn't the Tsar pleased!

"Well, Ivan—Young of Years, Old of Wisdom, you have done me a fine service indeed, and I praise you for it. Here is your reward: until now you were my Chief Groom. From this day I make you my Councillor."

At this the boyars and ministers frowned and they said to each other:

"A groom to sit among us! Such a disgrace! What can the Tsar be thinking of!"

But here the Self-Playing Psaltery struck up a tune, the Glee-Maker Cat began to sing and the Dancing Goose to dance. And there began such merriment that none of the noble guests could sit still, but they all jumped up and went into a dance.

Some time passed by, but they went on dancing. The kings' and tsars' crowns slid off to one side and sat askew on their heads, the

185

princes and tsareviches wheeled round and round in a squat, and the boyars and ministers sweated and gasped. On and on they danced and could not stop. And at last the Tsar waved his hand and begged:

"Stop the fun, do, Ivan—Young of Years, Old of Wisdom. We are all tired out!"

So Ivan put the three marvels away in a bag, and at once a quiet fell on the company.

The guests dropped down on the benches and sat there puffing and gasping.

"Now wasn't that a treat!" they cried. "Did anyone ever see the like of it!"

The kings and princes from foreign lands all envied the Tsar who was pleased as pleased could be.

"Now all the tsars and kings will learn about this and burst with envy," thought he.

"Not one of them has such wonders as these."

But the Tsar's bo-yars and ministers said to each other:

"If this goes on, the bumpkin'll be the first man in the tsardom soon. If we don't get rid of him, he'll give all the state offices to his bumpkin kinsmen, and he'll drive us, no-blemen, to death."

And so on the next day the boyars and ministers got together and sat thinking of a

way of ridding themselves of the Tsar's new Councillor. They thought and they thought, till at last one old boyar said:

"Let us call the drunkard, he's an old hand at such things."

They called the drunkard who came and bowed and said:

"I know what your honours want me for well enough. If you stand me a half-pail of wine, I'll teach you how to get rid of the Tsar's new Councillor."

"Speak up, and the half-pail is yours," said the boyars and ministers.

They gave him a cupful for a start and the drunkard drained it and said:

"It is forty years since our Tsar became a widower. Since then he has tried many times to woo Alyona the Lovely Tsarevna, but without success. Three times he waged war on her tsardom and lost ever so many soldiers, but he could not win her even by force. Let him send Ivan—Young of Years, Old of Wisdom after her. He will go, but will never come back."

The boyars and ministers took heart, and when morning came they went to the Tsar.

"How wise you were, Your Majesty, to find such a clever Councillor! It was no easy task to get the wonders he brought, but now he boasts he can carry off and bring you Alyona the Lovely Tsarevna."

When the Tsar heard the name of Alyona the Lovely Tsarevna, he couldn't sit still, but jumped off his throne.

"Now why didn't I think of it before!" he cried. "He is the very man to send after her."

He called his new Councillor and said:

"You are to go at once beyond the Thrice-Nine Lands to the Thrice-Ten Tsardom and fetch me Alyona the Lovely Tsarevna."

And Ivan—Young of Years, Old of Wisdom replied:

"But, Your Majesty, Alyona the Lovely Tsarevna is not the Self-Playing Psaltery, or the Dancing Goose, or the Glee-Maker Cat. You can't stuff her into a bag. Besides, she might not want to come here."

188

But the Tsar stamped his feet and waved his hands, and his beard shook.

"Don't you argue with me!" cried he. "I won't listen to any such talk. Do what you will, only bring her here. If you do, I shall give you a town to rule, with all the lands round it, and shall appoint you minister. But if you don't—I'll have your head cut off!"

Thoughtful and sad was Ivan when he left the Tsar. He began saddling his Mare with the Golden Mane, and the Mare asked:

"Why are you so sad and thoughtful, Master? Are you in trouble?"

"Not in any great trouble, no, but there's nothing to be pleased with, either," Ivan replied. "The Tsar has ordered me to fetch him Alyona the Lovely Tsarevna. He himself spent three years wooing her and all in vain, and he waged three wars to win her but could not, and now he sends me to fetch her all by myself."

"Oh, well, that's nothing to grieve about," said the Mare with the Golden Mane. "I'll help you, and we'll manage this between us somehow."

Ivan—Young of Years, Old of Wisdom didn't take long to get ready, and was soon off. And the last that folk saw of him was how he mounted his steed—none were quick enough to see him pass through the gate.

Whether he rode far or near, for a long or a little time nobody knows, but at last he came to the Thrice-Ten Tsardom, and a tall paling blocked his way. But his Mare with the Golden Mane leapt over it easily, and Ivan found himself in the Tsar's own garden.

Said the Mare with the Golden Mane:

"I shall turn myself into an apple-tree with golden apples, and you must hide beside me. Tomorrow Alyona the Lovely Tsarevna will come out for a walk, and she will want to pluck a golden apple. Now, don't you lose a minute when she's near but seize her, get on my back—I'll be ready at hand—and away we'll go. And mind, if you blunder, we'll both be dead."

189

On the following morning Alyona the Lovely Tsarevna came to the garden for a walk. She saw the apple-tree with its golden fruit and cried to her nurses, handmaids and chambermaids:

"Oh, look what a lovely apple-tree! And its apples are all gold! Stay here and wait till I go and pluck one."

Up she ran to the tree, and Ivan— Young of Years, Old of Wisdom jumped out as if from nowhere and he seized Alyona the Lovely Tsarevna. And that very minute the apple-tree turned back into the Mare with the Golden Mane, and she beat the ground with her hoofs to remind Ivan that he must make haste. And Ivan leaped into the saddle and drew Alyona the Lovely Tsarevna up with him, and that was the last her nurses, handmaids and chambermaids saw of them.

The women raised a cry, and the guards came running, but Alyona the Lovely Tsarevna was gone. The Tsar learned of it, and he sent out horsemen in all directions. But they all came back empty-handed. They had ridden their horses to death but had not even caught sight of the Tsarevna or the man who had carried her off.

Meanwhile Ivan—Young of Years, Old of Wisdom had galloped through many lands and left many lakes and rivers behind him.

At first Alyona the Lovely Tsarevna struggled and fought, but then she gave it up and wept quietly. She'd weep for a spell, and then look at Ivan, weep some more, and then look at him again. On the second day she spoke to him.

"Tell me, stranger," said she, "who are you and where do you come from? Where is your native land, and who are your kinsmen, and what is the name you go by?"

190

"My name is Ivan, and they call me Ivan—Young of Years, Old of Wisdom. I come from such and such a Tsardom, and my father and mother are peasants."

"Say then, Ivan—Young of Years, Old of Wisdom, have you carried me off because you want me for yourself or was it by anyone's orders?"

"It was the Tsar who ordered me to fetch you," said he.

At this Alyona the Lovely Tsarevna wrung her hands and cried:

"Never in my life will I marry that old fool! For three years he wooed me and couldn't win me: he waged three wars against my tsardom and lost a host of troops and couldn't get me; and he will not have me now, either."

These words pleased Ivan—Young of Years, Old of Wisdom well, but he said nothing and only thought to himself:

"If only I had a wife like that!"

By and by Ivan's own native land came in sight, and there was the old Tsar waiting for them on the front porch of his palace. Ivan—Young of Years, Old of Wisdom rode into the courtyard, and the Tsar scuttled down the steps, lifted Alyona the Lovely Tsarevna from the saddle and took her white hands in his.

"All these years," said he, "I've been sending my matchmakers and coming myself to woo you, and you've always refused. But this time you will have to marry me."

And Alyona the Lovely Tsarevna smiled wryly and said:

"You might let me rest from the journey, Your Majesty, before talking of marriage."

The Tsar bustled about and made a great fuss and he sent for the palace nurses, handmaids and chambermaids.

"Is her chamber ready for my most welcome guest, Alyona the Lovely Tsarevna?"

"It has long been ready, Your Majesty."

"Well, know then that she is to be your Tsaritsa, so do her bidding and obey her every word!"

191

Then the nurses, handmaids and chambermaids led Alyona the Lovely Tsarevna off to her chamber.

Said the Tsar to Ivan—Young of Years, Old of Wisdom:

"Well done, Ivan! For doing me this service you shall be my Prime Minister, and I bestow upon you three towns and all the lands round them."

A day passed and another, and the old Tsar grew ever more impatient, and longed to be wed. Said he to Alyona the Lovely Tsarevna:

"On what day is the wedding to be, when shall we go to church?"

And Alyona the Lovely Tsarevna replied:

"How can I be married when I haven't my wedding-ring or coach with me?"

"Oh, if that's all, it can't stop us," said the Tsar. "There are enough coaches and to spare in my tsardom, and rings too. You can have your choice. But if none of them please you, we can send a messenger to the lands beyond the sea to fetch you such as will."

"No, Your Majesty, I won't go to church in any but my own coach and I won't be wed with any but my own ring."

"And where may they be, your wedding-ring and your coach?"

"My ring is in my travelling trunk, my travelling trunk in my coach, and my coach near the Isle of Buyan, at the bottom of the Ocean-Sea. And until you get them, better not talk of marriage."

The Tsar took off his crown and scratched the back of his head.

"But how am I to get your coach from the bottom of the Ocean-Sea?"

"I don't care how you do it as long as you do it."

And off she swept to her own chamber.

The Tsar was left alone. He thought and thought till he remembered Ivan—Young of Years, Old of Wisdom.

"That's who will get me the ring and the coach!" said he.

And he sent straight for Ivan and said to him:

"Now, my faithful servant Ivan—Young of Years, Old of Wisdom, listen to what I say. You it was who got me the Self-Playing Psaltery, the Dancing Goose and the Glee-Maker Cat. You it was, too, who brought me Alyona the Lovely Tsarevna. Now do me a third service —bring me her wedding-ring and coach. The ring lies in her travelling trunk, the travelling trunk in her coach, and her coach, near the Isle of Buyan at the bottom of the Ocean-Sea. If you fetch me the ring and the coach, I shall make you lord over a third of my tsardom."

Said Ivan—Young of Years, Old of Wisdom:

"But, Your Majesty, I'm not a whale-fish. How can I go down to the sea bottom to look for the ring and coach?"

The Tsar flew into a temper, stamped his feet and shouted:

"None of that talk, now! Who's the Tsar here, you or I? It's for me to order and for you to obey! If you fetch me the ring and coach, I shall reward you royally; if you don't, then I'll have your head cut off!"

Off went Ivan to the stables, and he began saddling his Mare with the Golden Mane, and the Mare asked:

"Is it far you are going, Master?"

"I don't know myself yet, but go I must. The Tsar has ordered me to fetch him the Tsarevna's ring and coach. The ring lies in her travelling trunk, her travelling trunk in her coach, and the coach, near the Isle of Buyan at the bottom of the Ocean-Sea. And it is there we must go."

Said the Mare with the Golden Mane:

"This is a harder task than any that we have done so far. The way is not far, but it may end in woe. I know where the coach is, but it is not easy to get it. I shall go down to the bottom of the Ocean-Sea, and hitch myself to the coach. And I'll pull it out if the Sea-Horses don't see me. For if they do, they'll tear me to shreds, and you'll never see me or the coach any more."

At this Ivan—Young of Years, Old of Wisdom fell a-thinking. He thought and he thought, till at last he found a way out.

He went to the Tsar and said:

"I need twelve ox-hides, Your Majesty, twelve *poods* of tarred rope, twelve *poods* of tar and a cauldron."

"Take anything you want," said the Tsar, "only make haste and get on with your task."

Ivan—Young of Years, Old of Wisdom loaded the ox-hides, the rope and the big cauldron of tar on to a cart, hitched on his Mare and set out on his way.

They came to the seashore, to the Tsar's own meadows, and Ivan began covering the Mare with the hides and binding them with the rope.

"Even if the Sea-Horses do catch sight of you, they won't be able to bite through the hides so soon," said he.

And he wrapped the Mare up in all of the twelve hides and used up all the twelve *poods* of rope to tie them on with. Then he warmed up the tar and poured it on top—all the twelve *poods* of it.

"Now the Sea-Horses can't harm me," said the Mare with the Golden Mane. "Stay here in the meadows and wait for me for three days. Play on your psaltery and don't close your eyes."

And she plunged into the sea.

Ivan—Young of Years, Old of Wisdom was left all alone on the seashore. A day passed, and another, and still he kept awake, playing on his psaltery and keeping his eyes glued to the sea. But on the third day he began to feel drowsy, and even the psaltery couldn't help him. He struggled against sleep for a time, but it overpowered him at last, and before he knew it he had dozed off.

Whether he slept for a long or a little time nobody knows, but all of a sudden he seemed to hear the clatter of hoofs. He started up, and who should he see but the Mare with the Golden Mane bounding out on to the shore and pulling the coach behind her, while six golden-maned Sea-Horses hung to her sides.

Ivan—Young of Years, Old of Wisdom rushed towards her, and the Mare with the Golden Mane said:

195

"If you hadn't covered me with the ox-hides and tied and tarred them, you would never have seen me again. A whole herd of Sea-Horses fell on me. They tore nine of my twelve hides to shreds and bit through two others. And six of the horses got their teeth stuck so fast in the ropes and tar that they couldn't break loose. But that's all right, for you will find them useful."

Ivan—Young of Years, Old of Wisdom bound the Sea-Horses' feet so they could not run away and, pulling out his whip, set about teaching them reason. And as he flogged them he said:

"Will you take me for your master? Will you obey me? If you won't, I shall flay you alive and throw your carcasses to the wolves."

The Sea-Horses fell on their knees and began pleading with Ivan to spare them.

"Don't beat us any more, bonny lad," cried they. "We will obey your every word and serve you faithfully; and if ever you are in trouble, we shall come to your help."

So Ivan left off beating them and, hitching all seven horses to the coach, drove home. They dashed up to the front door of the Tsar's palace, and then Ivan took the Mare and the Sea-Horses to the stables and himself went to the Tsar.

"Come and take the coach, Your Majesty, it's waiting at your porch with all the dowry in it."

Out the Tsar rushed and straight to the coach, and he picked up the trunk and took it to Alyona the Lovely Tsarevna. But he did not say so much as a word of thanks to Ivan.

"Well, Alyona the Lovely Tsarevna," said he, "I have carried out all your wishes and whims. Here are your ring and trunk, and the coach stands waiting outside. Now say when the wedding is to be and for what day I am to invite the guests."

Said Alyona the Lovely Tsarevna in reply:

"I don't mind marrying you, and we can have the wedding soon. But I don't like being seen going to church with anyone so old and grizzly. What will people say? They'll surely laugh at us: 'Look at that old man marrying a young girl!' they'll say. 'Doesn't he know what he is letting himself in for! Why, he'll only be doing other men a favour.' And gossips' mouths are hard to stop, you know. Now if only you grew younger before we married, all would be well."

"Nothing would please me more," the Tsar said. "But you must teach me how to do it. It's something no one has heard of in our tsardom."

"You must take three big copper cauldrons and fill one with whole milk and the other two with spring water. The cauldron with milk and one of the cauldrons with water should be heated, and just as they start boiling, you must first jump into the milk, then into the hot water and last into the cold. And when you have had a dip in all of the three cauldrons, you will come out as young and handsome as a man of twenty."

"But won't I get scalded?" asked the Tsar.

"In my tsardom there are no old people at all. Everyone does it, and no one ever got scalded."

So the Tsar went and had everything made ready as Alyona had

told him. But when the milk and water came to the boil he was frightened and couldn't make up his mind to jump in. He walked round and round the cauldrons, and then he slapped his forehead and said:

"What can I be thinking of! Let Ivan—Young of Years, Old of Wisdom have a bathe first, and if it all comes out well, I shall dive in myself. If not, and he gets scalded, I won't have lost anything. All his horses will be mine, and I won't have to share my tsardom with him as I promised."

And he sent for Ivan—Young of Years, Old of Wisdom.

"What is it you want, Your Majesty?" Ivan asked. "Why, I haven't even rested from my journey yet."

"I will not keep you long—just take a dip in these cauldrons and then go and rest," said the Tsar.

Ivan looked into the cauldrons. The two with the milk and water were seething and boiling, and only in the third was the water calm and cool.

"You don't want to boil me alive, Your Majesty, do you?" he said. "Is that your reward for my faithful service?"

"Oh, no, Ivan. You see, if an old man takes a dip in them he becomes as young and handsome as a man of twenty."

"But I'm not old, Your Majesty, I don't need to get any younger."

The Tsar was angry.

"Dear me, what a fellow you are to argue! Always ready to cross me! If you don't jump in of your own free will, I'll have you thrown in. I see you want to taste the rack, my lad!"

Just then Alyona the Lovely Tsarevna ran out from her chamber and, catching a moment when the Tsar was not looking, whispered to Ivan:

"Tell your Mare with the Golden Mane and the Sea-Horses that you are going to do it before you dive in. Then you may bathe without fear."

And to the Tsar she said:

198

"I came to see if everything had been made ready for you as I told you."

And she went up to the cauldrons and looked in.

"I see it is all as it should be," she said. "Have your bathe now, and I will run off to get ready for the wedding."

And off she went to her chamber. Ivan—Young of Years, Old of Wisdom shot a look at the Tsar and said:

"Very well, I shall do as you say one last time. One can only die once. But let me go and have a last look at my Mare with the Golden Mane. It may be the last time I see her, and we've travelled far and long together."

"Very well, you may go, but don't be long there."

So Ivan—Young of Years, Old of Wisdom went to the stables and told his Mare and Sea-Horses everything.

"When you hear us snort three times," said they, "dive in and fear nothing."

Ivan went back to the Tsar.

"I'm quite ready now, Your Majesty," he said, "I'll dive in right away."

Just then the horses gave three snorts, and in he went with a splash into the hot milk. Then he dived out and plunged into the hot water, and last he dipped into the cold water. And he came out of the third cauldron as handsome as the sky at dawn, the handsomest youth that ever was born.

The Tsar saw him and wavered no more. Up he scrambled on to the platform, plunged into the milk, and was boiled alive.

Alyona the Lovely Tsarevna hurried down from the porch and took Ivan—Young of Years, Old of Wisdom by the hands and slipped her ring on his finger.

Then she smiled and said:

"You carried me off by order of the Tsar, but he is dead, you may do as you will: if you like, you may take me back; and if not, you may keep me for yourself."

199

And Ivan—Young of Years, Old of Wisdom took her white hands in his and called her his own dear bride and slipped his ring on her finger.

After that he sent messengers to his village to call his mother and father and his brothers to the wedding. And soon after his mother and father and the thirty-two bonny lads, his brothers, came to the palace.

And then they were wed and there was a grand feast, and Ivan—Young of Years, Old of Wisdom and Alyona the Lovely Tsarevna lived happily ever after and took good care of Ivan's mother and father.

The Seven Simeons—Seven Brave Workingmen

O nce upon a time there lived seven brothers, seven brave workingmen, and they were all named Simeon.

One day, they went out into the field to meet the morn and the sun to greet, to plough the soil and to sow some wheat, and it so happened that, at that very time, the Tsar and his *voyevodas*, the grandest of his noblemen, chanced to be riding by. The Tsar looked and, seeing the seven brothers, was much surprised.

"What can it mean?" said he. "Seven youths are ploughing one field, and they are all the same height and look alike too. Find out who they are."

And the Tsar's servants ran and brought before him the seven Simeons—seven brave workingmen.

"Well, now, tell me who you are and what you do tor a living," the Tsar demanded. And the seven brothers replied:

"We are seven brothers, seven brave workingmen, and we are all called Simeon. We plough the land that was our father's and his father's before him, and in addition each of us has been taught a trade of his own."

"Who has been taught to do what?" asked the Tsar.

Said the eldest brother:

"I am Simeon the Carpenter and Blacksmith, and I can make a pillar of iron reaching from the ground to the very sky."

Said the second brother:

"I am Simeon the Climber, and I can climb to the top of that pillar and look to all sides to see what goes on where."

Said the third brother:

"I am Simeon the Sailor, and I can build a ship in the wink of an eye, and sail her over the seas and under the water too."

"I am Simeon the Archer," said the fourth brother, "and I can hit a fly in the air with my arrow."

"I am Simeon the Astrologer," said the fifth brother, "and I can count the stars and never miss a single one of them."

"I am Simeon the Ploughman," said the sixth brother, "and I can plough a field, sow the grain and reap the harvest all in one day."

"And what can you do?" asked the Tsar of the youngest of the seven Simeons.

"I can sing and dance, o Tsar good father, and play on a pipe," the youth replied.

At this one of the Tsar's *voyevodas* said spitefully:

"Workingmen we need, o Tsar good father, but what do we want with a fellow who can do nothing but dance and play! Send him away, for such as he are not worth the bread they eat or the *kvass* they drink."

"You may well be right," agreed the Tsar.

And the youngest of the Simeons bowed to the Tsar and said:

"Allow me to play for you and show what I can do, o Tsar good father."

"Very well," said the Tsar, "play for me just once and then leave my tsardom!"

The youngest of the Simeons took out his pipe of birch bark and started playing a Russian dance tune, and at once everyone who was there and could hear him went into a dance and began to skip and prance. The Tsar danced, and the boyars danced, and the guards. The horses in the stalls frisked and capered, the cows in the sheds stamped in time to the music and, in the hen-house, the hens and roosters hopped about gaily. But the *voyevoda* danced harder than anyone. In fact, so hard did he dance that the sweat rolled down his face, and the tears too, and his beard jerked and shook.

"Stop your playing, I can't dance any longer, I'm all in and fit to drop!" cried the Tsar in loud tones.

Said the youngest of the Simeons:

"Rest now, good folk, all but you, *voyevoda*. I'll make you dance some more for your spiteful tongue and evil eye."

And at once everyone stood still, all but the *voyevoda* who went on dancing and could not stop. He danced and danced till at last his legs buckled under him, and he sank to the ground and lay there, opening and closing his mouth like a fish out of water.

Said the youngest of the Simeons flinging aside his pipe of birch bark:

"And that, Tsar, is my trade!"

The Tsar laughed at this, but the *voyevoda* was ill pleased and plotted revenge.

"Well, now, Simeon the Eldest, show us what you can do!" said the Tsar.

And the oldest of the Simeons took a hammer weighing all of fifteen *poods* and forged a pillar of iron reaching from the ground to the blue sky above.

Then the second Simeon climbed up on to the pillar top and began to look to all sides.

"Speak and tell us what you see!" the Tsar called to him.

And the second Simeon called back:

"I see ships sailing the sea, I see wheat ripening in the fields."

"What else do you see?"

"On the Ocean-Sea an isle I see. 'Tis the Isle of Buyan gleaming bright in the sun. And there, at the window of a palace of gold, sits Yelena the Beautiful weaving a silken rug."

"What is she like? Is she really as beautiful as they say?" asked the Tsar.

"That she is. Indeed, such is her beauty as cannot be pictured and cannot be told but is a true wonder and joy to behold. She wears the crescent moon for a crown, and each hair on her head is agleam with pearls."

Now this made the Tsar eager to have Yelena the Beautiful for his wife, and he was about to send his matchmakers to her when the wicked *voyevoda* said, trying to set him against the seven Simeons:

"Why do you not send the seven Simeons after Yelena the Beautiful, o Tsar good father! They are skilful and clever and should be able to succeed in the venture. And if they fail, you can have their heads chopped off for them."

"Yes, that's a good idea!" said the Tsar.

And he ordered the seven Simeons to bring him Yelena the Beautiful.

"If you don't," said he, "then I swear by my sword and my tsardom whole that off your shoulders your heads will fall!"

It could not be helped, so Simeon the Sailor took an axe, and rap-tap! he built a ship in the wink of an eye, fitted her out and rigged her, and launched her too. They loaded the ship full with goods of every make and kind, the costliest gifts that they could find, and the Tsar ordered the wicked *voyevoda* to go with the brothers and see that they did as they were bade. The *voyevoda* turned white, but there was nothing to be done. Do not dig a pit for others if you do not want to fall in yourself.

They boarded the ship, and at her sides the billows lapped, and in the wind the sails flapped, and then they gathered way and set sail across the Ocean-Sea for the Isle of Buyan that gleamed bright in the sun.

Whether they sailed for a long time or a little time no one knows, but at last the island lay before them.

They stepped out on shore, went straight to Yelena the Beautiful and, laying at her feet the costly gifts they had brought, began to plead with her to bestow her hand upon the Tsar.

Yelena the Beautiful took the gifts, and, as she was looking them over, the wicked *voyevoda* whispered in her ear:

"Do not marry the Tsar, Yelena the Beautiful. He is old and feeble, and in his tsardom the wolves howl and the bears prowl."

Yelena the Beautiful flew into a temper and ordered the matchmakers out of her palace.

What were the seven brothers to do?

"Listen to me, my brothers," said the youngest of the seven Simeons. "You go on board the ship and prepare to weigh anchor. Put in a supply of bread and hoist the sails, and leave it to me to fetch Yelena the Beautiful."

And lo! before the hour was up Simeon the Ploughman had ploughed up the sandy shore, sowed some rye, gathered in the harvest and baked enough bread to last them the whole journey back. They hoisted the sails and began to wait for Simeon the Youngest.

Simeon the Youngest went to the palace, and there was Yelena the Beautiful seated at the window weaving a silken rug. So he sat down on a bench beneath the window, and spoke thus:

"It is beautiful here in your realm in the middle of the Ocean-Sea, on the Isle of Buyan that gleams bright in the sun, but it is a hundred times more so in Rus, my own dear motherland. Our rivers are blue and our birches are white; our fields are vast and our meadows are green and bright with flowers. In Rus, sunset meets sunrise and the crescent moon in the sky keeps watch over the stars. Our dew is as sweet as honey, and our streams gleam like silver. In the morning the shepherd will walk out on to the green meadow and put his pipe of birch bark to his lips and, whether you want to or not, you will follow wherever he leads."

Simeon the Youngest began playing on his pipe of birch bark, and Yelena the Beautiful stepped out on to the threshold of gold. He played on, and started across the garden, and Yelena the Beautiful went after him. Simeon crossed the garden, and Yelena the Beautiful trailed behind him. He traversed the meadow, and she followed in his wake. He walked on along the sandy shore, and there she was at his heels. He went on board the ship, and so did she.

And now the brothers hastily pulled up the gangplank, turned round the ship and set sail across the blue sea.

Simeon the Youngest stopped playing on his pipe, and at once Yelena the Beautiful came to and looked round her. All about was the Ocean-Sea, and the Isle of Buyan gleaming bright in the sun was left far behind.

Yelena the Beautiful threw herself down on to the pine floor, and then, turning into a blue star, she streaked up into the sky and was lost among the other stars. But Simeon the Astrologer came running out, he counted all the bright stars in the sky and he found the new star. And now Simeon the Archer rushed out on deck and he shot a golden arrow up at the star. And the star rolled down on to the pine floor and turned into Yelena the Beautiful again.

Said Simeon the Youngest:

"Do not try to run away, Yelena the Beautiful, for there is nowhere you can hide from us. But if you dislike our company, then we had better take you back to your Isle of Buyan that gleams bright in the sun, and let the Tsar chop off our heads for us."

Hearing him, Yelena the Beautiful felt very sorry for Simeon the Youngest.

"No," said she, "they shall not chop off your head because of me, Simeon the Piper. You may take me to the Tsar."

They sailed for a day, and they sailed for another day. Simeon the

209

Youngest never left the Tsarevna's side, and she could not tear her eyes off him.

But the wicked *voyevoda* took note of it and hatched an evil plot.

They were nearing home, and already the shore was in sight, and the *voyevoda* called the brothers out on to the deck and offered them a cup of sweet wine.

"Let us drink to our homeland, friends!" said he.

The brothers drank the wine and, stretching themselves out on the deck, fell fast asleep. Now the *voyevoda* had put a sleeping potion in the wine, and nothing, neither thunder nor storm, nor their mother's tears flowing tender and warm, could wake them.

Only Yelena the Beautiful and Simeon the Youngest, who had not touched the wine, stayed awake.

They reached the shore, and still the six brothers slept and did not wake. Simeon the Youngest began preparing to take Yelena the Beautiful to the Tsar, and both of them wept and sobbed, for it broke their hearts to part from one another. But it could not be helped, for a rule that all good folk accept is that a promise must be kept.

Meanwhile, the wicked *voyevoda* ran to the Tsar and, prostrating himself before him, said:

"O Tsar good father, Simeon the Youngest is plotting against you. He wants to kill you and take Yelena the Beautiful for himself. Have him put to death."

Simeon the Youngest and Yelena the Beautiful now appeared before the Tsar and, after showing the Tsarevna into the palace with all the honours due her, the Tsar ordered Simeon to be put in prison.

"Hear me, my brothers, hear me, six Simeons!" cried Simeon the Youngest. "Come to your youngest brother's aid."

But the brothers slept on and did not wake.

210

Simeon the Youngest was thrown in a dungeon and fettered with iron chains and, at the break of day, he was led out and taken to where the headsmen were waiting to chop off his head.

Yelena the Beautiful wept, the tears rolling like pearls down her cheeks, but the wicked *voyevoda* laughed spitefully.

Said Simeon the Youngest:

"O Tsar, you who are without mercy, before I die, grant me my last wish, for so our ancient custom bids you do. Allow me to play on my pipe for the last time."

"Don't do it, o Tsar good father, don't let him play!" cried the wicked *voyevoda*.

But the Tsar said:

"I shall not go against the customs of our fathers. Play, Simeon, but make haste, for my headsmen have waited too long, their sharp swords have blunted."

And Simeon the Youngest put his pipe of birch bark to his lips and began to play.

Across hills and across dales the music carried and the strains of it reached the ship where slept the six brothers and woke them.

"Our youngest brother must be in trouble!" cried they, starting to their feet.

And off they set at a run for the Tsar's court.

The headsmen had just grasped their sharp swords and were about to chop off Simeon's head, when, lo and behold! as if out of thin air the six brothers appeared: Simeon the Carpenter, Simeon the Climber, Simeon the Ploughman, Simeon the Sailor, Simeon the Astrologer and Simeon the Archer.

They moved in a body upon the old Tsar and they said in threatening tones:

"Free our youngest brother, Tsar, and give up Yelena the Beautiful to him!"

212

The Tsar was frightened and said:

"Take your youngest brother, and the Tsarevna too, and be quick about it. I do not like her much, anyway."

After that Simeon the Youngest and Yelena the Beautiful were married, and such a feast was held as the world had never seen. They drank their fill and ate their fill, and they sang merry songs with great good will.

Then Simeon the Youngest took his pipe and began playing a cheery dance tune.

The Tsar danced, and the Tsarevna danced, the boyars danced and their ladies danced too. The horses in the stables frisked and pranced, the cows in the shed stamped in time to the music and, in the hen-house, the hens and roosters skipped about gaily.

But the *voyevoda* danced harder than anyone. He danced till his legs gave under him and he fell to the ground, dead.

All good things have an end and, now that the wedding and feast was over, it was time to go back to work again.

And work they did!

Simeon the Carpenter built houses, Simeon the Ploughman sowed wheat, Simeon the Sailor sailed the seas, Simeon the Astrologer kept count of the stars, and Simeon the Archer guarded Rus from her enemies. There was enough work and to spare for all in this great good land of ours.

And, as for Simeon the Youngest, he sang songs and played on his pipe, and his music warmed the people's hearts and lightened their labour. For all who heard him sing and all who heard him play, waxed cheerful and bright for the rest of the day!

CPSIA information can be obtained at www.ICGtesting.com
Printed in the USA
LVOW11s2007060114

368315LV00001B/257/A